FRIEND
OR FOE?

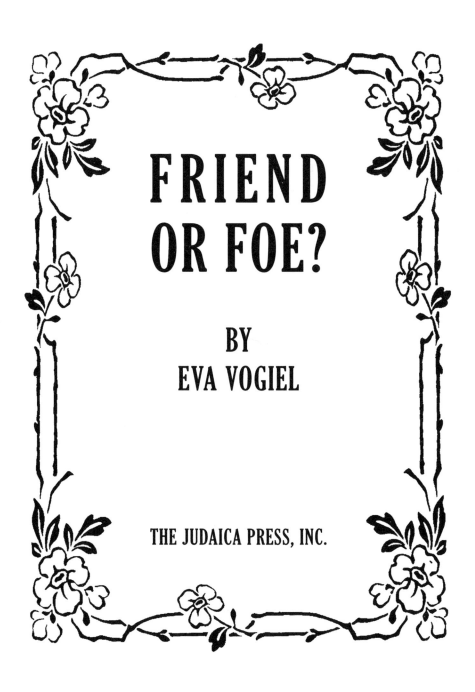

FRIEND OR FOE?

BY
EVA VOGIEL

THE JUDAICA PRESS, INC.

ISBN 1-880582-66-X

THE JUDAICA PRESS, INC.
718-972-6200   800-972-6201
info@judaicapress.com
www.judaicapress.com

Manufactured in the United States of America

TABLE
OF CONTENTS

ACKNOWLEDGEMENTS

START THIS ACKNOWLEDGEMENT WITH THANKS to the *Ribono Shel Olam* for giving me the *siyata dishmaya* to complete another book.

I would also, once again, like to thank all the members of my family and all those friends and advisors who have given me so much help and encouragement.

I am grateful to the Imperial War Museum for sending me pictures and information on the bombs used by the Germans in World War II.

Thanks to Barbara Weinblatt, managing editor of The Judaica Press, and to Bonnie Goldman, who worked on editing this book. I am also grateful to Zisi Berkowitz for her book design, and Shira Kovacs and Chana Leah Hirschhorn for their superb assistance in producing my book.

Finally, I must not forget all my readers, young and old, (and in between!) who are, after all, the reason for putting pen to paper!

Many thanks and may Hashem bless you all!   E.V.

SURPRISE
REUNION

HEN Migdal Binoh school reopened for its second year, in September, 1948, the main topic of conversation was the sudden appearance of Nechy Horowitz's mother.

Everyone in the school was talking about it. And the fact that Nechy herself was not there made it easy for tongues to wag.

"Have you heard? Nechy's mother suddenly turned up in London one day."

"Yes, that's right! Nechy had the shock of her life! She thought her mother was dead! And her mother didn't know that Nechy was alive. Can you imagine!"

"Oh, really? I heard that her mother had come to London especially to look for her."

That was the gist of most of the conversations buzzing amongst the groups of girls. The dramatic story took many twists and turns, as no one knew the true facts.

No one, that is, except Mrs. Langfeld, the headmistress,

who had been correctly informed, and Mrs. Langfeld's daughter, Etty, who had been told a little and had actually overheard the rest.

While they were unpacking their belongings in the dormitory, Etty wasted no time furnishing her roommates with all the details. Needless to say, the unpacking process was considerably slowed down as the girls listened, spellbound, to the amazing story.

"You all know that Nechy's mother was in a concentration camp," Etty told them, full of self-importance. "Well, by the time they were liberated, she was so weak and ill that she was taken straight to a hospital in Germany. Later, she was moved to another hospital in Vienna. She was suffering from some sort of illness and for almost two years she just lay there, more dead than alive. Quite gradually, however, *Baruch Hashem*, she began to recover and regain some of her strength.

"Soon Mrs. Horowitz began to call for her children. It was tragic, really. She kept asking the hospital staff to find her three children for her. The nurses, though sympathetic, were convinced there was little chance of any of them still being alive. So many people had been killed. They wouldn't say that to *her*, of course, so they humored her and pretended they would try to trace them. In the end, Mrs. Horowitz became so insistent, they did get in touch with someone to make inquiries. It was discovered that Nechy's older brother and sister had indeed been killed." Etty lowered her voice at this point, an expression of sympathy and horror on her face, which was reflected on the faces of her audience. "But Nechy—who had been hidden by non-Jewish friends—had been placed with a children's transport. After quite a long time, Nechy was traced in London.

"Once Mrs. Horowitz knew where her daughter was she insisted on coming to London to find her. The doctors didn't think she was fit enough to travel because she was still ill. They finally had to let her go because she fretted so much that it was hampering her progress. The *Agudah* organized her trip to London and arranged for somewhere for her to stay and even provided a generous stipend.

"They knew that Nechy went to school here, but, of course, it was the middle of the summer holidays. So they contacted Mummy to ask where Nechy was. Mummy knew that Nechy and Shulamis were staying with Yitty Lieber and she offered to break the news to Nechy herself. She phoned the Liebers and was told that Nechy had gone out for the day with Shulamis and Yitty. Mrs. Lieber said she would give Nechy the news as soon as she came back, but Mummy didn't think it would be a good idea. The Liebers' household is always so busy and hectic and Mummy thought she ought to be told in quieter surroundings.

"So she left a message that Nechy should come to our house. Of course," Etty sighed, "I was sent out of the room when Nechy came, so I don't really know how she reacted when she was told. But she looked sort of dazed and astonished when she came out. Mummy took her straight round to the house where her mother was. Oh, how I wish I could have been there and seen their reunion! It must have been so amazing! Mummy didn't tell me much, but she said it was incredibly emotional, as you can imagine!"

"I can imagine," Etty's friend, Reisy Lerner, commented. "She must have been thrilled to pieces…once she got over the shock!"

"I wonder if she's ever going to come back to school," Miriam Bloom pondered. "I bet she won't want to leave her mother's side!"

"Yes, but she might come back," Etty said. "Her mother is still quite weak and she may even have to go to a nursing home for a while. She wasn't really well enough to leave the hospital. She just insisted because she wanted to see Nechy!"

"I wonder how the other three refuge girls feel about all this," Shanni Beckman mused. "I bet they're wondering if *their* mothers are going to turn up too, one day."

It was obvious which "other three" she was referring to. Nechy Horowitz had been part of a foursome—four young orphaned refugee girls who had all been brought to London during the war and had been cared for in a hostel for refugees, until they had come to the newly-opened Migdal Binoh School.

"It's hardly likely," Etty remarked. "Yocheved and Chaya actually saw their parents being killed." Involuntarily, a shudder went through her at the thought of those gruesome events, "And as for Shulamis…well, I'm not sure, but I think she knows what happened to her parents, too."

The discussion was brought to an abrupt halt by the shrill sound of the bell. A wave of panic swept through Dormitory Six.

"Help!" Goldie Feldman cried, "I haven't finished unpacking yet and we're supposed to be downstairs for the assembly in five minutes!"

"Well, never mind," Etty said, hastily stuffing a few things into her locker in a haphazard manner. "Push everything in and we can straighten out later on. Come on, let's go!"

Mingling with the stream of girls emerging from the other dormitories, they made their way down the stairs to the Assembly Hall, where Mrs. Langfeld was waiting to welcome them.

Etty felt immensely proud as she listened to her mother speak in her clear, authoritative voice to the group of students assembled.

She seemed a different person from the heartbroken,

defenseless woman she had been in 1941, when her husband, Aryeh, had been killed during an air raid, leaving her with three young children. Of course, she still felt her loss, Etty knew...she still missed her father too...but opening this school seemed to have made Mrs. Langfeld more confident and self-assured. Now that her children had grown up—her son, Nochum Tzvi, was married with a son of his own; her daughter, Bayla, was doing well at Gateshead Seminary, and Etty, now fourteen, was beginning to mature, too—running Migdal Binoh provided Mrs. Langfeld with the sense of purpose she needed.

Welcoming the new pupils to the school and giving them a rough outline of the rules, she greeted all the girls warmly and expressed the hope that they would all pull together, as before, to make the school's second year as successful as the first year had been. She spoke a few more words of *chizuk* and then dismissed them.

"You can all do as you please for the rest of the afternoon," she said. "You can stay indoors or out, as long as you remain on the school grounds. But before you do anything I suggest you all go straight to the dining room for tea and some delicious chocolate cake that Mrs. Hoffman has prepared!"

Mrs. Langfeld could not help smile at the expressions of delight emanating from the girls at the mention of Mrs. Hoffman's cake. The school's Hungarian cook prepared astonishingly tasty delicacies for special occasions.

Making her way toward the dining room with Reisy, Etty encountered Yocheved Levinsky talking to her friend, Frumie Kleiner, in the hall.

"Hi," she greeted them. "How were your holidays?"

"Great!" Yocheved replied. "Isn't it wonderful about Nechy's mother?"

There was genuine pleasure in Yocheved's voice and Etty

regarded her with admiration and relief. Yocheved was obviously not envious in the least, even though she knew there was no chance of *her* mother ever reappearing.

"Yes, it's super!" Etty agreed and moved on.

In the dining room Etty made a bee-line for the table, where most of the girls had gathered, eager to grab a piece of Mrs. Hoffman's delicious cake. On the way, she bumped into Shulamis Berenstock.

"Oops! Sorry!" Shulamis exclaimed. "Hi, Etty!"

"No, *I'm* sorry," Etty said. "Hello, Shulamis!" She eyed the girl with interest. Shulamis and Nechy had both arrived at the same time in England as war orphans, when they were five years old. They had been inseparable ever since. They were really as close as sisters. Etty could not help wondering how Shulamis felt about Nechy's situation. Although she was not sure if she was being tactless, Etty fumbled around for the right way to broach the subject.

"You must miss Nechy a lot," she tentatively suggested.

"Yes, terribly!" Shulamis replied, shaking her head of dark, curly hair expressively. Essentially a bubbly, happy-go-lucky type, it was unusual for her to look so serious. "I'm ever so happy for her—really I am! It's just that I feel a bit lost without her."

"Why? Isn't she coming back? I thought she probably would."

"Yes, I think she is. But it won't be quite the same, somehow." There was a note of wistfulness in Shulamis's voice for a moment. "Oh, come on!" Shulamis said suddenly, her natural effervescence rising to the surface. "Let's go and get some cake before there's none left!"

When Etty went into her mother's office to say "goodnight" before going to bed, she recounted the conversation she had had with Shulamis.

"She really didn't seem jealous at all. I'm sure she's ever so happy for Nechy, but I can't help feeling sorry for her. Yocheved and Chaya have got each other and Nechy's now got her mother, but who has Shulamis got? Nechy was like a sister to her."

"I'm sure they'll still be very close," Mrs. Langfeld said.

"Mm," Etty was thoughtful. "What happened to Shulamis's parents, Mummy? Do you know?"

"Yes, I'm surprised you don't know. It's no secret. Shulamis was an orphan before the war. Her parents were both killed in some sort of accident—I'm not quite sure what. Shulamis was two or three years old at the time and doesn't really remember them. She was looked after by her grandparents. When the war started they sent her away on a children's transport. They both decided to stay behind in Vienna and, unfortunately, neither of them survived. I actually remember them slightly. They had a bakery shop." A faraway look came into Mrs. Langfeld's eyes as she remembered her own youth in Vienna, before she had come over to England in 1924 as a young bride.

"Oh, poor Shulamis!" Etty's voice was full of sympathy.

"Yes," her mother said, "but *Hashem* has given her a special gift. She's such a lively, optimistic person. I'm sure her sunny nature will be a terrific advantage to her throughout her life!"

NEW NEIGHBORS

"**H**ey, Etty! Do you see what I see?" Reisy cried, pointing excitedly. She and Etty were taking a leisurely stroll down the lane and had reached "The Willows," an attractive 18th-century cottage, referred to at Migdal Binoh as "the house next door." Technically, it was the house next door, but, since the school building was a large mansion, set in extensive grounds, the next house was actually quite a few yards down the lane.

Reisy was pointing to a "For Sale" notice that had been perched near the gate for the last seven months. The word "SOLD" had been pasted in bold letters over the place where "For Sale" had stood.

"Someone must have bought it during the holidays!" Etty observed. "I'm so curious to know who it is."

"I hope it's someone as nice as old Mr. Butterworth," Reisy said.

"Well, it won't be someone as old, anyway," Etty commented. "He only moved out to live near his son because he was too old to live on his own."

"I wonder if the new owners will putter about in the garden as much as he did?" Reisy mused, surveying the overgrown lawn and the neglected flower beds. "He was so proud of his garden—and look at it now!"

"Whoever it is, they obviously don't mind a school with a bunch of noisy girls next door," Etty reflected. "Mr. Butterworth's daughter-in-law once complained to Mummy that they can't sell the house because of us. She said people only buy houses in the country because they want a bit of peace and quiet."

"That's not fair!" Reisy exclaimed, shaking her mop of dark, frizzy hair indignantly. "It's not as if we make a lot of noise!"

"I know, but prospective buyers don't know that! They just hear the word "school" and it puts them off. I suppose they had to put the price down a lot and someone couldn't resist a bargain! Anyway," Etty began to quicken her pace, "let's hurry back. I can't wait to tell Mummy!"

It was not long before the news about a new neighbor had spread round the whole school and it soon replaced Nechy's mother's miraculous appearance as the main topic of conversation.

Unable to contain their curiosity, the girls constantly made excuses to go outside so that they could hover around near the cottage.

For a week nothing seemed to be happening. Then, one day, toward the end of mid-morning break, three third-formers came rushing into the school grounds, announcing that they could see a large moving van down the road. There was a sudden stampede as many girls began to rush out, eager to see for themselves. However, just as the first girl reached the gate, the bell rang out loudly, summoning them back to the classrooms.

With groans of disappointment, they turned back, telling themselves—and each other—that it would probably be there for most of the day and they would still have a chance to see it after dinner.

The news soon reached Mrs. Langfeld's ears and, realizing that the girls would no doubt throng near the cottage, trying to catch a glimpse of the new inhabitants of "The Willows," she walked into the dining room at dinner time and announced that nobody was to go out of the school grounds that day.

"The last thing we want," she said, "is for our new neighbors to be faced with a large crowd of inquisitive schoolgirls staring at them. It will make a *terrible* impression—not to mention a *chillul Hashem*."

The girls knew that Mrs. Langfeld was right, of course, but they could barely conceal their disappointment. So while they had been rushing their meal in their hurry to get out, they now ate slowly and unenthusiastically.

Later that afternoon, when they had gathered in the Assembly Hall to *daven minchah*, the headmistress broached the subject again.

"I can't forbid you all to go out into the street from now on," she said. "All I can do is ask you to use your common sense. I know you are all extremely curious to see what the people who have moved in are like, but we must avoid antagonizing them! I don't want any complaints that girls are hanging around near their cottage, staring at them. Is that clear?"

There was a murmur of assent and most of the girls did, indeed, heed her words. There were, however, some overly curious girls who could not resist the temptation. These girls came back and reported what they had seen to their own groups of friends.

"They were both sitting in the front garden," third-former Mindy Spiegel told a crowd of avid listeners. "They looked sort of oldish, about sixty, I think. He's got gray hair and a moustache and she's got curly whitish-blonde hair—permed and dyed, if you ask me."

Another girl reported seeing the man mowing the lawn. "He's sort of medium height and quite plump," she told *her* friends.

Even the teachers seemed interested and discussed the matter amongst themselves in the staff room.

Mrs. Langfeld, although mildly curious herself, had little room to spare in her thoughts for the new neighbors. Her mind was occupied with a disturbing telephone conversation she had had with Nechy Horowitz a few days earlier. Expecting the girl to sound happy and elated, she detected a distinct note of strain and tension in Nechy's voice.

"I'm coming back to school after Sukkos, *im yirtzeh Hashem*," Nechy had told her. "It is all right, isn't it? I mean, I am expected, aren't I?"

"Of course you are! We'll be glad to see you back…especially Shulamis. You know she's missing you so." There was an audible sigh at the other end of the line. Poor thing, Mrs. Langfeld thought, she probably feels bad for her friend. "She's so happy for you!" she assured her hastily. "In fact, everybody is. The whole school is buzzing with excitement!"

There was another deep sigh and the headmistress began to feel alarmed. "Is everything all right, Nechy? How is your mother?"

"*Boruch Hashem* she's doing well, but the doctor says she needs a few months in a nursing home so she will be going to one in Chingford."

There was silence for a long minute. Then Nechy suddenly blurted out, "Oh, Mrs. Langfeld! I feel so awful leaving her!"

"I'm sure it will do her a world of good," Mrs. Langfeld said encouragingly. "So you mustn't worry about her. The best thing for you is to come back to school now."

"Yes," Nechy sounded hesitant.

"Nechy, please think about it. There is no reason why you shouldn't come back to school! Your mother is in good hands…and you can always go down to see her in Chingford from time to time if you want to."

"I know…but it's not that…" there was a strange edge to Nechy's voice. "I feel guilty for *wanting* to come back."

"But Nechy," Mrs. Langfeld began when she was interrupted by three pips on the telephone, signifying her money in the public telephone had run out.

"Oh, my time's up!" Nechy said. "Bye, Mrs. Langfeld! See you next week." They were suddenly cut off and Mrs. Langfeld was left staring at the receiver, a puzzled expression on her face.

It was ironic that Mrs. Langfeld, who showed the least interest in the new owners of "The Willows," should be the first to meet them face to face. A few days after the worrying conversation with Nechy, the telephone rang in the headmistress's office.

I hope it's not Nechy again, saying she's not coming, Mrs. Langfeld thought as she picked up the receiver.

"Hello," she said, a little nervously, "Migdal Binoh School."

"Could I speak to the headmistress please," an unfamiliar man's voice came across the line.

"Speaking."

"Oh." The voice sounded slightly taken aback. He had obviously expected a secretary to answer. "My name is Gerald Campbell. My wife and I have just moved into the cottage down the lane. Well, next door to you really."

"Our new neighbors!" Mrs. Langfeld, composing herself quickly, put a welcoming note into her voice. "It's so nice to hear from you!"

"Likewise!" Mr. Campbell replied.

"We've seen some of your pupils going past…"

Here goes! Mrs. Langfeld thought, a complaint already! "I hope they're not making a nuisance of themselves," she said defensively.

"Oh no! On the contrary! They all seem perfectly charming! The fact is, Miss…er," Mr. Campbell hesitated for a moment.

"Langfeld. Mrs. Langfeld," the headmistress informed him.

"Ah yes, now I remember—the agent did tell us your name. Well, Mrs. Langfeld, since we are neighbors, my wife and I are anxious to introduce ourselves and make your acquaintance. When do you think it would be convenient for us to call on you?"

In truth, Mrs. Langfeld was quite busy with organizing all the students back into the school after their time off and she didn't have a lot of time to visit with her neighbors. Furthermore, too many of the girls would be hovering around, agog with curiosity, and the visit would be given more importance than it merited. However, she knew she had no choice but to be cordial so as not to cause a *chillul Hashem*. Mrs. Langfeld thought for a moment and chose a time when all the girls were at lessons but she herself was free.

"Shall we say tomorrow at two-thirty?" she suggested.

"Fine," Mr. Campbell said. "We'll be there!"

Mrs. Langfeld received her guests in the reception room. As she poured the tea for them she scrutinized them intently. They were an odd-looking pair. Mr. Campbell was average in height and stockily built. His iron-gray, wavy hair was well plastered down with hair oil but his eyebrows, unkempt and untreated, stood out bushily over slightly bulging mid-brown eyes. Under a pointed nose with dilated nostrils he sported a neatly trimmed moustache. His somber charcoal-gray waistcoat suit, black and maroon bow-tie and bowler hat, which he had placed on the seat next to him, made him look out of place in the English countryside. No doubt he'll change that soon, Mrs. Langfeld reflected, for the tweed jacket and deerstalker hat everyone seems to wear round here.

His wife, Emily, made Mrs. Langfeld think of a garment that had been washed too many times. Everything about her seemed colorless. Her eyes were pale blue and her hair, dyed ash-blonde, was frizzy and styleless. She wore a lilac and white floral dress, with a cameo brooch at her neck, which she fingered nervously from time to time.

Mr. Campbell was doing most of the talking and as Mrs. Langfeld listened to him, she tried to identify the slight accent that was present in his speech.

"I was born in Scotland," he was saying. "Naturally, I wanted to settle there when I retired, but Emily's worried about the climate."

Aha, he's Scottish, Mrs. Langfeld thought. That explains the accent.

"Well, it doesn't stop raining there!" Mrs. Campbell protested plaintively. "Everyone knows it's warmer down

South. And this is such a picturesque village, isn't it?" She selected a piece of cake from the plate on the table as she spoke and bit into it. "Mm! This cake is *absolutely* delicious! Where did you buy it? I have had no luck finding a good bakery in the neighborhood. I must go and get some!"

"Oh, everything here is homemade," the headmistress informed her. "Mrs. Hoffman, our cook, bakes and cooks beautifully!"

"Really? I must get the recipe from her! I don't bake much as a rule, but for a cake like this it's worth making the effort!"

Mrs. Langfeld smiled wryly at the thought of Mrs. Hoffman giving one of her precious Hungarian recipes to this English woman. Mrs. Hoffman was so possessive of her recipes.

"Yoy! What a waste!" she could almost hear the cook saying. "Never, *never* will she be able to bake it properly!"

"Mrs. Langfeld," Mr. Campbell regarded the headmistress shrewdly, "what was it you said this school is called? It was some unusual name, I seem to remember."

"Migdal Binoh. It's Hebrew."

"Oh?" The bushy eyebrows shot up. "What does it mean? And why do you have a Hebrew name for your school?"

"Literally translated it means 'Tower of Understanding,'" Mrs. Langfeld explained. "And the answer to your second question I should have thought was obvious. We chose a Hebrew name because this is a Jewish school."

"I see. So that means you have mainly Jewish pupils here?"

"Actually, they are all Jewish!" the headmistress explained.

"But what do you do if non-Jews apply for admission?" Mr. Campbell asked.

"We refuse them."

"And the authorities allow it?" There was surprise in the man's voice.

"The 'authorities' are not consulted. It has *nothing* to do with them, since this school is self-supporting. We don't receive a penny from any authorities!"

"But still," Mr. Campbell argued, "it must be against their principles. Children are supposed to mix and integrate. In my opinion—"

"—Opinions differ, Mr. Campbell!" Mrs. Langfeld interrupted him. She had no desire to explain to him that the Jewish people had a different way of life and therefore could not integrate into English society. He didn't seem like he would understand, in any case.

She stole a surreptitious glance at the clock on the wall. There was still half-an-hour till her *Chumash* lesson with Form *Vov*. She would give the Campbells another twenty minutes and if they had not gone by then she would have an excuse to end this unnerving interview. There was something about their line of questioning that made her feel under attack.

Mr. Campbell was questioning her again. "Do you and your husband live on the premises, Mrs. Langfeld?"

"My husband was killed during the war," Mrs. Langfeld told Mr. Campbell. "The place where he was doing fire-watching duty was hit by a bomb."

"Oh, how sad!" Emily Campbell's fingers fiddled nervously with her brooch.

Mrs. Langfeld sighed. "Yes, it was a terrible shock, even though we knew it was something that could happen. I suppose you must have felt the same anxiety whenever your husband was on duty, Mrs. Campbell." She was aware of Mrs. Campbell shifting uncomfortably in her seat. "I suppose he was also in the army during the war," she added.

"Yes, Gerald was in the army," Mrs. Campbell said, glancing at her husband, who nodded, a guarded look in his eyes.

He must have dodged all his duties, Mrs. Langfeld thought, and now they are both ashamed of it! Oh well, it's none of my business.

She stood up. "I do hope you'll excuse me," she said politely. "I've enjoyed meeting you and I would love to continue talking to you, but I'm due to give a lesson in ten minutes."

"Oh, sorry to have kept you!" Mrs. Campbell apologized, as they both stood up.

"Not at all. It's been a pleasure!" Mrs. Langfeld said, hoping she sounded convincing. "Thank you so much for coming."

"What subject do you teach?" Mr. Campbell asked, as he walked toward the door, replacing his bowler hat on his head.

"Religious studies," the headmistress replied.

"Really? How interesting! Is that what you have your degree in?"

"Well…no, not really," Mrs. Langfeld said, feeling uncomfortable.

"Then what is?"

"The fact is…I don't actually have a degree. I didn't go to university."

"And yet you are the headmistress here? I must say, that does surprise me!" Mr. Campbell stared at her for a long moment, his bushy eyebrows raised, then he shrugged. "Well, good day, Mrs. Langfeld. Thank you for your hospitality. As neighbors, I daresay we will be seeing quite a lot of each other."

Mrs. Campbell echoed his thanks. "And please ask your cook if I can come in sometime for that recipe," she added.

Mrs. Langfeld saw them out and went into her office to collect her books for the lesson. For some reason, she felt a strange uneasiness. Looking back on the conversation she realized that the man had asked rather a lot of questions. It reminded her of the school's first term, when a stranger had appeared at the gate and asked questions. That had eventually led to some of the girls being kidnapped!

Mrs. Langfeld did not really think Mr. Campbell was up to anything quite so sinister. But she had a definite feeling that there was a streak of anti-Semitism behind that friendly facade. It was a good idea to take no chances, she told herself, and resolved to be constantly on her guard!

AN INTANGIBLE BARRIER

SHULAMIS SAT UP IN BED AND LISTENED. Something had awoken her—some sound—but her mind, still a little befuddled from sleep, could not quite identify it. Yes, there it was! She could hear a girl sobbing. It was pitch dark in the dormitory and, as her eyes had not yet become accustomed to the darkness, she had to rely on her sense of hearing to tell her where it was coming from. Soon she was in no doubt that it was from the bed next to hers…Nechy's bed.

Filled with consternation, she lay still for a moment, wondering what to do. Here was another piece of the puzzle that was baffling Shulamis ever since Nechy's return.

When Shulamis had heard that Nechy was coming back to school she had been happy and excited, but as soon as she set eyes on her friend she had been shocked by the change in her. In appearance she was still the same; slightly built with ginger hair and freckles; but the hitherto placid, easy-going manner had left her. Her eyes now had a haunted look and her usual spontaneous smile was no longer there.

Perplexed and concerned, Shulamis had tried to reach out to her but her attempts to draw her out were unsuccessful. A strange barrier had come down between them, making it impossible to get through to Nechy and find out what was troubling her.

And now, Nechy was sobbing quietly to herself and Shulamis was not sure whether to approach her or not. Nechy might well snub her or at any rate be embarrassed to have been found out. But, Shulamis resolved, as she noiselessly slipped out of bed, a friend *is* a friend and Nechy needed her, even if she would not admit it right now.

"Nechy," she whispered urgently, hoping she would not wake any of the other girls in the dormitory, "what is it? Please tell me what's the matter!"

The sobbing ceased abruptly and Nechy began to take deep breaths, obviously attempting to give the impression that she was asleep.

Somewhat put out, Shulamis hovered hesitantly for a few moments. Then, with a resigned shrug, Shulamis returned to her bed. If that was the way Nechy wanted it, she told herself, then there was nothing she could do.

But, as she lay listening to Nechy's artificial breathing, she wondered if she had given in too easily. Perhaps Nechy really did want to talk to her. Should she try again? No, she decided, the dormitory was not the right place. Some of their roommates might wake up and overhear their conversation. Tomorrow, she resolved, she would make another attempt at inducing her friend to open up to her.

Unable to fall asleep, Shulamis let her mind wander back to the day, a few weeks ago, when Nechy had come back from her reunion with her mother.

Starry-eyed, Nechy had entered the Liebers' garden and joined Shulamis on the bench.

"Oh, Shulamis!" she had cried, "You know how much I've dreamt about this happening! But I never ever really thought it would ever come true!"

"I'm so happy for you, Nechy!" Shulamis declared, hugging her friend tightly as tears ran down her face.

Nechy, too, had been crying softly and together the girls sobbed for a few minutes. They had been best friends for so long. This moment had long been awaited.

Then Nechy pulled away and a sober expression had crossed her face suddenly.

"But Shulamis, I feel so awful!" she said, flushing. "Here I am all excited and going on about it, while you…" She stopped, embarrassed.

"Don't be silly!" Shulamis reassured her, "it's different for me. I don't even remember my mother, so I couldn't very well dream about her. But I'm so excited for you that your dream has come true, really I am!"

"I know you are…and thanks," Nechy regarded her warmly. Then she sighed. "I wish she looked more like the mother I remember," she said solemnly. "She's so thin and pale, I hardly recognized her. And on top of that, we could hardly talk to each other…and there was so much I wanted to say!"

"Why couldn't you talk?" Shulamis asked.

"Because Mummy doesn't understand a word of English, and I can hardly speak anything else these days!"

"Well, what language were you used to speaking? You came from Belgium, didn't you?"

"Yes, I was born in Belgium," Nechy said, "but my family

only settled there in 1935, just before I was born. They came originally from Czechoslovakia. At home, we spoke only Yiddish, but since I have come here I've forgotten most of it. I can understand it more or less, but I can't really converse fluently in Yiddish!"

"Oh, yes, that must be a problem," Shulamis sympathized. She shook her head. How really awful it was to not to be able to communicate properly!

"Never mind!" Nechy said positively, her smile returning. "I'll manage somehow!" She looked thoughtful for a moment, as if trying to conjure something up in her memory. "Do you remember Matty and Layka?"

"Of course," Shulamis replied, remembering the two older girls who had been at the refugees hostel with them. "They were always speaking Yiddish, weren't they?"

"That's right! So I do remember quite a few words and I'm jolly well going to learn the rest!" There was determination in her voice and a sparkle in her greenish-blue eyes.

"Where are you both going to live?" Shulamis asked. "Are you going to stay in London?"

"I suppose so. It's too early to talk about it. Mummy still needs so much medical care…there was talk of her going to a nursing home for a while. I expect I'll be coming back to school, though I don't know when. Meanwhile, I'm moving into the Myersons tomorrow, to be with her."

"Oh…" Shulamis's face fell. "I'll miss you," she said softly.

"Oh, Shulamis! I'll miss you too." There was a note of sadness in Nechy's tone. "We've been closer than sisters all these years. Oh, how I wish you could come with me. Hey, you know what?" she said, brightening up suddenly. "When Mummy's better and we have a place of our own, maybe you could come and live with us! Perhaps Mummy might even adopt you! Then we'd really be sisters!"

Shulamis laughed at her enthusiasm, but she felt a little embarrassed. The last thing she wanted to do was intrude.

Now, lying in the dark and thinking about it, she could hardly believe that conversation had taken place. What had happened to change Nechy's attitude so completely? Only a short while ago she had been on top of the world, and they were still best friends. What had made her drop to the depths of despair? And why had she withdrawn from a friend whom she herself had said was like a sister? Somehow, Shulamis knew, she must get to the bottom of it!

Getting Nechy alone proved harder than Shulamis had imagined. Nechy seemed to be avoiding her. But Shulamis doggedly persisted to seek opportunities to find a private moment and, eventually, her efforts were rewarded. Lessons were over for the day and Nechy had taken her tea outside and settled herself on a bench, ready to do some homework and catch up on the work she had missed. Shulamis spotted her and went over to her immediately.

"Mind if I join you?" she asked.

"Sure," Nechy moved up to make room for her, her manner friendly. But there was wariness in her eyes.

"Nechy," Shulamis began, deciding to charge straight in. "What was the matter with you last night? Why were you crying?"

"Crying? Me?" Nechy sounded puzzled, but she avoided her friend's gaze. "You must have imagined it."

"No, I didn't! Don't you remember? I even came up to you and asked you what was wrong!"

"Did you?" Nechy began to shuffle her books about, her eyes still averted. "And what did I say?"

"You didn't answer!" Shulamis said, almost accusingly.

"Well, there you are then!" Nechy said, triumphantly, looking up at last, "I was fast asleep! I was probably having a nightmare."

Shulamis was about to disagree when Nechy spoke quickly, obviously trying to steer her away from the subject.

"Guess what? I saw the new neighbors today. They look a bit weird, don't you think?"

Shulamis wasn't fooled. Nechy had not shown the least bit of interest in the new owners of "The Willows" since she had come back.

"Don't change the subject!" Shulamis said, hoping she was not being too aggressive. "Nechy, what's happened to you? You've changed and I know something is worrying you. I want to help you, but I can't if you won't tell me what it is!"

"You can't help me anyway," Nechy's voice dropped to a whisper. "*Nobody* can."

"But I'm your best friend!" Shulamis protested. "You know how much I care about you!"

Nechy turned to face her, her greenish-blue eyes filled with tears. "Shulamis," she said in a serious and terribly sad voice, "don't probe! I *can't* tell you…and you wouldn't understand in any case. I know you mean well, but please…*leave me alone!*" Nechy stood up, gathered her books and her cup and plate, and walked away, leaving Shulamis on the bench, a look of utter astonishment on her face.

What had she done? Where had she gone wrong? Now she was sure she had driven Nechy even further away, and the knowledge hurt deeply. Nechy was her very best friend in the whole world! Shulamis had no one she was as close to. Now she was suddenly, absolutely alone in the world! They had been so close since they were both five years old. Closer than sisters, even, since they each had no sisters, parents or other relatives. Shulamis desperately searched her mind for ways to remove this huge barrier that had suddenly come between them. If she only knew what was causing it! She could then find some way to tear the barrier down. But how could she tackle something that was so obscure?

As she mulled over her options she realized she badly needed someone's advice, but whom could she talk to? Yocheved Levinsky? In some ways Yocheved was like a big sister, since she was the oldest of this odd group of four orphans who had been together since arriving in England in 1940. But, even though Yocheved was the most levelheaded and sensible of the four, would she really know what to do? And was it fair to burden her, when she had problems of her own, as well as having her younger sister, Chaya, to worry about?

No, Shulamis decided, she would have to talk with an adult. In that case, she may as well go straight to the top. Mrs. Langfeld, besides being quite understanding, really seemed to care about the girls as much as a mother would. Shulamis resolved that she was definitely the best person to speak to.

It was with growing concern that Mrs. Langfeld listened to Shulamis. She, too, was worried about the change in Nechy, but she had hoped that once Nechy got back into the swing of things at school, the tension would leave her. Now, hearing that she would not even communicate with her closest friend, the headmistress realized that the situation was more serious than she had thought.

She looked at Shulamis, whose usually cheerful countenance and clear brown eyes were clouded with worry and anxiety. She wished she could reassure Shulamis and solve the problem for her. But it seemed there was no easy solution.

"We've got to give her time," Mrs. Langfeld told Shulamis. "Perhaps the problem is one that will resolve itself. And if not, I'm sure Nechy will eventually come to terms with it."

"But I feel she needs my help!" Shulamis cried vehemently. "And I can't bear the way she's shut me out!"

With this, tears of hurt began streaming from Shulamis's bright eyes.

"You must not let it hurt you, Shulamis," Mrs. Langfeld said kindly, feeling compassion for this strong-willed young woman. "She doesn't mean it that way. It's because she feels close to you that it upsets her to know that you don't understand."

"But how does Nechy know I wouldn't understand if she doesn't even try talking to me? I've never ever had a problem understanding her before!"

"Perhaps it's because she doesn't quite understand it herself, so she may feel that nobody else can understand." Mrs. Langfeld placed a hand on the girl's shoulder. "Showing your eagerness to understand her only makes her more frustrated. Don't try to draw her out. Why not just let her know you support her by simply being there? When she really feels the need to talk to someone she'll be glad of your presence."

Mrs. Langfeld's tone had a soothing effect on Shulamis. Besides, it felt so good to have let her feelings out and to know that Mrs. Langfeld understood her. So, somewhat reassured, Shulamis left the headmistress's office, determined to play her cards right and gain Nechy's confidence once more.

Mrs. Langfeld watched Shulamis leave her office and sighed. She hoped what she had said was true and Nechy would come back to her old self soon. However, she was fully aware that a person can become deeply entrenched within a self-made brick wall. She knew that she, too, must do her best to help Nechy and she prayed for *siyata dishmaya* (heavenly assistance) to ensure that she did the right thing.

Her eye fell upon the letter on her desk. Mrs. Langfeld had been reading it when Shulamis had knocked, and now the interview she had had with her accentuated the nagging worry the letter incurred.

They needed this school, these four orphan girls…as well as most of the other pupils. Thinking back, Mrs. Langfeld realized how many people had benefited through Migdal Binoh. There had been the Kleiner girls, Frumie and Judy—sisters who had endured a terrible accident, only to come to resolution by the end of the year. Not to mention Madame Debrett, the French and art teacher. Coming to the school had changed the course of her life too. And Mrs. Langfeld herself? Where would she have been without the school?

Picking up the letter she read again the menacing words, telling her that a government inspector would be calling on the school to assess the school and make sure that it met with their requirements.

Mrs. Langfeld tried to push the alarming thought out of her mind, but it persisted in coming to the forefront. What if the inspector was not satisfied with what he saw? He would surely demand the closure of the school!

TENSE MOMENTS

T HE SCHOOL INSPECTOR WALKED OUT THROUGH the front door, his portfolio under his arm, and turned round briefly. With a nod and a smile he raised his hat slightly and, turning back, made his way toward his car. It was the first time he had smiled since he had arrived, at nine o'clock that morning, and Mrs. Langfeld was not sure whether it was a good sign or not. All day, as she had escorted him from one classroom to the next and watched as he examined exercise books and studied last year's test results, she had looked out for some indication of approval. But the inscrutable mask never left his freckled face.

She watched him drive away in his blue car and closed the door, letting out a long, drawn-out sigh. The day had been so tense that she felt drained and exhausted. All she wanted now was to sit quietly in her comfortable office and try to unwind.

It was therefore with mixed feelings that she spotted Etty walking toward the office, a cup and saucer in her hand. They reached the door at the same time.

"Mummy, you look exhausted!" Etty said, concern on her face. "I've brought you a cup of sweet tea. I'm sure you could do with it!"

"Etty! How sweet of you!" Mrs. Langfeld exclaimed, moved by her daughter's thoughtfulness. Perhaps it was a good idea after all. Maybe talking to Etty would be the tonic she needed right now... better for her than sitting by herself and brooding. "Why don't you come into the office and let's sit together for a moment!"

Etty followed her mother into the office and set the pink tea cup down on the wooden desk, watching Mrs. Langfeld sink wearily into her chair and begin to sip the tea. The drawn look on the her mother's face filled Etty with misgivings. Things did not look too good!

"Well?" Etty asked impatiently. "What did the inspector say?"

"Nothing much," her mother replied vaguely.

"But he must have said something! Was he satisfied or not? Please tell me! I can't stand the suspense any longer!"

Mrs. Langfeld sighed. "Etty, dear, please calm down! You'll just have to be patient, like the rest of us. I really have no idea what he thought. All he told me was that he's going to make out a report and that I would probably hear from them in about a week."

"A week! That's ages!" Etty cried. "I'll go mad with worry till then!"

In spite of herself, Mrs. Langfeld smiled. "I hope you won't," she teased. "All I need is a mad daughter on my hands! Look," she said more seriously, "we're all on edge about it, but worrying won't help. We just have to have *bitochon* that things will turn out all right. I can't see why he shouldn't approve. You've all done a great job and everyone's grades and test scores were excellent!"

"Yes, you're right about having *bitochon*," Etty said, standing up. "After all, we've all been saying *Tehillim* every day, and we'll go on saying them! So relax, Mummy, and don't worry!"

"Thanks, Etty, for your excellent advice," Mrs. Langfeld said with mock solemnity, amused at Etty's typical habit of turning the tables.

Etty left the office and made her way to the common-room, where Reisy was waiting to review French vocabulary with her. On her way she met Nechy.

"Hi, Nechy!" she greeted her cheerily, wishing Nechy would smile in response. Nechy's strange, uncharacteristic behavior these days was most disconcerting!

"Etty, has the inspector gone?" Nechy asked immediately, anxiety in her tone.

"Yes, he left about half-an-hour ago. Why do you want to know?"

"I saw you go into the office. Tell me," Nechy pleaded, "what did your mother say? Was he satisfied?"

"Mummy doesn't know. He didn't tell her anything. We'll only know in about a week."

"Oh…" Nechy was thoughtful for a moment. "I hope they won't close the school!" she blurted out suddenly.

"Yes, we all do," Etty agreed.

"I know, but for me it's not only school. It's my home!" Nechy said this quite dramatically.

Etty regarded her quizzically. "But Nechy, now that your mother's come back you'll soon have a proper home."

Nechy appeared to be making an effort to pull herself together and it seemed to Etty as if a veil had suddenly come down over the girl's freckled face.

"Yes, yes…you're right. Of course I will! Well, I'd better get on with my homework," she said quickly and hurried away.

Etty stared after her, mystified. What was going on? Who

would have believed that Nechy—calm, placid, outgoing Nechy—would turn into this miserable, withdrawn, almost neurotic girl? And to make matters worse, it was clearly affecting Shulamis, too. Although still bubbly and vivacious, Shulamis wasn't quite as happy-go-lucky as usual. Etty had lately observed her often regarding Nechy with a worried frown.

Etty sighed. In this school, another complication seemed to crop up every minute! She marveled at the way her mother managed to cope with it all. She would never be able to run a girls' boarding school, she told herself, with all the tensions and problems it entailed, and all of the different personalities. But Mummy always seemed to understand the girls and to know just what to do. If, *chas veshalom*, the local authorities decided to close the school, it would be such a waste of a good headmistress!

Although the days since the inspector's visit passed quite quickly, the tense atmosphere in the school remained. Mrs. Langfeld tried not to think about it as she kept herself busy with the everyday running of the school, but it was difficult to push it out of her mind. She was not sure whether she wanted the week to be over or not. The suspense was hard to take but, as long as she had heard nothing, she could, at least, live in hope.

Two days before the week was up, when the telephone rang in her office, Mrs. Langfeld answered it, quite calm and unsuspecting. It was only when she heard the official-sounding man's voice on the line that her hand began to tremble.

"This is it!" she told herself, vaguely surprised that she would be given notice by telephone and not by letter, but convinced, nevertheless, that that was what was coming.

"Mrs. Langfeld?" the voice said. "This is Horace Dobson, chairman of the West-Buckinghamshire Education Committee."

"Oh, yes!" Mrs. Langfeld was glad he could not see her passing her tongue over lips that had suddenly gone dry…not to mention her shaking hand.

"I've studied the inspector's report," Mr. Dobson said. (Could he hear the loud thumping of her heart, Mrs. Langfeld wondered?) "And there are one or two points I would like to discuss with you. Would it be all right for me to call some time this morning? What time would suit you best?"

This morning! Mrs. Langfeld was tempted to acquiesce, even though it would mean rearranging her lessons. She yearned to put an end to this agonizing uncertainty. But she was reluctant to rearrange any lessons. The upheaval would not be very good for the girls.

"Not this morning—preferably," she said. "I will be giving lessons for most of this morning and changing them around would cause too much disruption. The interest of my pupils has to come first, you understand."

"Quite commendable," Mr. Dobson commented.

"But I am free this afternoon," Mrs. Langfeld went on, "if that would be convenient for you."

A time was fixed for that afternoon and Mrs. Langfeld replaced the receiver, her mind in a whirl. What was all that about? she wondered. Did she dare hope that it was a good sign? After all, "discussing a few points" hardly sounded as if he intended to close the school. On the other hand…

Oh well, speculating would get her nowhere. She would have to get through the morning somehow and she had better not let her mind dwell on it too much or her lessons would suffer.

When, at last, the appointed time came and the doorbell rang, Mrs. Langfeld went to answer it and tried her hardest to appear cool and calm.

The man standing at the door almost matched the mental picture his voice had conjured up in her mind. Short, stout and round-faced, he sported a dark handle-bar moustache and wore gold-rimmed spectacles almost at the end of his nose. He bowed slightly and raised his brown hat stiffly. When he spoke, his voice sounded even more pompous than it had on the telephone.

"Mrs. Langfeld?" he inquired. "Mrs. Minna Langfeld?"

"Yes," the headmistress replied, wondering if he thought there might be two Mrs. Langfelds and he wanted to make sure he was not speaking with the wrong one. "Please come in."

She ushered him into the office, asking him if he would like a cup of tea. It occurred to her that a slice or two of Mrs. Hoffman's delicious cake might put him in a good mood! But what's the difference, she reflected. The decision, whatever it was, had already been made!

Mr. Dobson refused the tea, saying he would like to get straight down to business.

"Yes...of course," Mrs. Langfeld said apprehensively.

"As you know," Mr. Dobson began, opening his black leather briefcase and taking out a document, "our inspector, Keith Warren, was most impressed by your high standards."

"He was?" Mrs. Langfeld interrupted, the relief showing in her face. "I didn't know."

"You didn't?" Mr. Dobson eyed her over the top of his spectacles. "He really should have given you a rough outline of his findings. But that is typical of our Mr. Warren!" he spoke with the tone of an indulgent schoolmaster discussing a naughty pupil. "Always keeps his thoughts to himself. It must be the result of his working for the Secret Service during the war! However," he reverted to his business-like tone, "that is neither here nor there. As I said, it seems your standard of education is exceptionally high, not to mention your excellent test results. Mr. Warren was also most impressed by the behavior and manners of your girls."

Mr. Dobson's eyes traveled down the page as he spoke in an impassive voice. "As to the general condition of these premises, he found the standard of hygiene most satisfactory and the accommodations adequate at the moment. However, should your school expand further, as is likely, there is danger of overcrowding." He looked up. "You may be requested to find a larger building, or to extend this one, in which case you could possibly qualify for a grant. Furthermore, although that is not our department, you would have to apply to the Elmsleigh Council for planning permission."

Mrs. Langfeld was jubilant! So, there was no danger to the school after all! She hadn't realized how tense and worried she had been. She felt as if a huge weight had been lifted off her shoulders. But Mr. Dobson's next words sent her elation plummeting once more.

"There is just one thing," he said. "I am given to understand that you, as headmistress, have no university degree or qualifications. Is that correct?"

Mrs. Langfeld stared at him.

How did he know that? What did he mean by "given to understand?" But who had told him? Mr. Warren had asked no questions concerning qualifications.

Someone else must have told him.

"Mr. Dobson," she said, trying not to show that she was upset, "how do you know that I have no formal qualifications?

I can't remember at any time being asked about them!"

"Oh, so it's not true," Mr. Dobson looked relieved.

"No, I didn't say that. As it happens, it is true. But, since this is a private school and my salary is not paid by your committee, I do not see whose business it is!"

"B-but there are certain government requirements," Mr. Dobson began, stammering a little.

"In that case, why was I not asked about it when an application was made for permission to open this school?"

The color rose in Mr. Dobson's face and he tugged, somewhat nervously, at his moustache. He would not admit it to this dignified headmistress, but she was right. At the time, he had not been chairman of the committee, but a mere clerk in the department and the application had been his responsibility. He was the one who should have checked the headmistress' qualifications and he had, in fact, overlooked it. It was a good thing no one else was aware of the oversight, or things could be quite awkward for him. He had better say no more about it.

"Well…hmm…Mrs. Langfeld," he said, shifting uncomfortably, "since you have acquired such a high standard here and are running this school so admirably, I am prepared to overlook this matter for now. However, should we find, at next year's inspection, that your standard has fallen below the required level, we might have to think again." He tried to give Mrs. Langfeld a stern look, but his embarrassment seemed to show through.

When, after another stiff bow, Mr. Dobson took his leave, Mrs. Langfeld allowed herself time to ponder. As relieved as she was at the outcome of the interview it bothered her how Mr. Dobson came to find out that her qualifications were not up to government standards. Who could have told him? She herself had never volunteered the information. And Sir Isaac

Greenhorn, the school's benefactor, who had given in the application, did not know either and would surely have checked with her, had he been asked.

She suddenly remembered that she ought to immediately telephone Sir Isaac and give him the good news that the school was not to be axed after all. She would ask him about it at the same time.

"I'm delighted to hear it!" Sir Isaac said when Mrs. Langfeld had reached him. "Though I never really worried that it would happen! There isn't a better school in the country!"

"Thank you," Mrs. Langfeld said, gratified.

"Sir Isaac, can I ask you something?"

"Certainly. What is it?"

"When you applied for permission, did they ask you anything about my qualifications?"

"No," came the reply. "I didn't even know you had any, but I would have checked with you if I'd been asked."

"Actually, I haven't got any…" Mrs. Langfeld told him.

"So? What does it matter? You're doing an absolutely brilliant job and in any case, it's a private school so it's nobody's business."

"It's not quite as simple as that," Mrs. Langfeld said, "but never mind that just now. I just wonder who told them."

"It wasn't me," Sir Isaac informed her. "Well, thank you for letting me know the good news, Mrs. Langfeld. I couldn't be more pleased! May you have continued *hatzlachah* in the future! May you go from strength to strength!"

Mrs. Langfeld thanked him and hung up. But her puzzled expression remained. As she mulled over the mystery, she remembered that the only person to whom she had spoken of the matter was their new neighbor, Mr. Campbell. But he was a relative stranger in the village and hardly knew anyone. He couldn't have been the one to mention it. Or could he?

PUTTING PRESSURE ON NECHY

"**H**ERE ARE SOME MORE ENTRIES FOR THE magazine," Yocheved Levinsky told her friend, Frumie Kleiner, waving a pile of papers toward her. "It's *Cheshvan* already, so we ought to get on with it. Shall we go up to the office and sort them out now?"

"Okay," Frumie agreed. "I've done my geography homework already, so I've got a bit of time."

Together, the two girls made their way up the stairs toward the little office they used to edit and produce the school magazine. The main editor of the magazine was Suri Bernstein, but since she had moved up to the sixth form, she was too occupied studying for her exams to give much time to the magazine. She had therefore delegated most of the responsibility to her two younger co-editors. They made a perfect team, these two girls. Yocheved, bespectacled, with straight brown hair, was studious and excelled in most of the school subjects. Dark-haired Frumie was quite tall and slim and she, too, had a serious air about her. Her exceptional flair for the English language was a great asset to the magazine.

They reached the room, situated at the end of a long, narrow corridor, and Yocheved took out the key Suri had entrusted her with.

"Come on," Yocheved said as they entered the tiny office, "let's get straight down to work. You look through this lot and I'll look through these." She handed Frumie half the bundle of papers she was holding.

"Right," Frumie said, taking the papers from her and sitting down.

"We've got quite a lot of material this time. But there's not a single illustration yet. Have you spoken to Nechy?"

"Yes. I don't know what's happened to Nechy lately." Yocheved looked perturbed. "She seems to have lost all her enthusiasm. I can see something's bothering her, but I don't know what it is. You'd think she'd be on top of the world now!"

"Perhaps she's feeling a kind of delayed shock," Frumie suggested, playing the amateur psychologist. "After all, all this was sprung on her so suddenly. She was taken completely by surprise."

"You might be right," Yocheved said pensively, "but it's all so unlike her! And I thought I knew her so well! Oh well," she sighed, "it looks as if we'll have to manage without her illustrations. Do you think your sister Judy can be persuaded to illustrate the whole magazine?"

Frumie looked doubtful. "I don't know," she said. "She's working on the cover and you know her. She's such a perfectionist, she takes her time over it. Besides, I think she'd feel she was trespassing on Nechy's territory. It would be a shame if Nechy doesn't do them. Her illustrations are so good!"

"I know," Yocheved agreed. "And I'm sure it's not good for her to give up doing them. She needs things to keep busy. You know," she said suddenly, on a more definite note, "I think we ought to pressure her. It may be hard for her to break out of this lethargic state she's in but I'm sure she'll be a lot happier once she's done it. This might be just the boost that she needs!"

"Oh I hope you're right," Frumie said with feeling. "I hate seeing her like this! You'll have to be the one to speak to her though. She's more likely to take it from you. I'm not that close with her."

"Well, I'll try," Yocheved sounded hesitant, "but I'm not much good at persuading people."

"Oh no?" Frumie laughed teasingly. "I haven't forgotten the way you talked *me* into helping with the magazine!"

"Well, that was different. You really *wanted* to be talked into it!" Yocheved said, smiling confidently.

"So how do you know that Nechy doesn't?" Frumie argued. "She may just be waiting for someone to push her a bit. And you're pretty good at that!"

"On the other hand she could resent it," Yocheved said uncertainly. "The last thing I want to do is antagonize her. Still," she gave a resigned shrug, "nothing ventured, nothing gained. I'll definitely give it a try. Wish me *hatzlachah*!"

The next day was Tuesday, the day when all the classes from Form *Daled* upwards had the afternoon off. As soon as lunch was over and the girls, having *bentched*, were making their way out of the dining room, Yocheved waylaid Nechy at the door.

"Nechy, are you busy this afternoon?"

"No, not really," Nechy looked apprehensive. "Why?"

"I wondered if you fancied coming for a stroll," Yocheved said. "There's something I'd like to discuss with you."

There was unmistakable wariness in Nechy's greenish-blue eyes. Yocheved was sure Nechy would have liked to find some excuse, but it was too late. She had already said she wasn't busy.

"All right," Nechy said in a noncommittal voice. "Is it important?"

"Yes, actually, it's quite important," Yocheved told her.

They strolled out into the school grounds where, here and there, a few red and gold autumn leaves had fallen across well-mown lawns. The girls made their leisurely way toward the gate in silence. Yocheved seemed deep in thought and Nechy kept eyeing her with growing uneasiness.

Presently, as they began to amble down the lane, Yocheved opened the conversation. "How is your mother, Nechy?" she asked.

Nechy looked startled. Surely Yocheved hadn't taken her out for a walk just to ask her that! *Boruch Hashem,* she's doing well," she answered in a strangely detached voice. "At least I hope she is. I'm going to Chingford over Shabbos to see her."

"Oh, that's good!" Yocheved smiled encouragingly. "I hope you'll see a big improvement. But Nechy...when you come back, do you think you'll be able to make a start on those illustrations? We really need you. We want to start duplicating the magazine soon and we can't till you've done some illustrations."

"Oh!" Nechy bit her lip and looked at Yocheved apologetically. "I'm sorry. I know I'm letting you down, but it's no use! I just can't do them! Please ask someone else...Judy Kleiner, for instance, can do a super job."

"Judy can't do them all. And besides, your drawings are so good. Everybody loves them! The magazine just won't be the same without them!"

Nechy smiled wanly. "Thank you, Yocheved. It's nice of

you to say so. But I tell you, I just can't draw anymore! I seem to have lost the talent!" There was a wild look in her eyes.

"Nonsense!" Yocheved could not conceal her annoyance. "People don't just lose their talent!" She threw an irritated look at Nechy, but, noticing tears in her eyes, was immediately contrite. "Oh Nechy, I'm sorry! I didn't mean to shout at you! But it's true what I said. A talent doesn't go away. It's inborn in a person. So you can't have lost yours!" Her voice softened as she adopted a persuasive tone once more. "I wish you'd give it a try. I'm sure it will all come back to you. And we're depending on you…"

"Oh, now you're making me feel guilty!" Nechy said plaintively. She looked down at the ground and kicked away a stone, watching as it bounced out of sight. Presently Nechy looked up and faced her companion, a look of frustration on her face. She was obviously fighting an inner battle. "All right," she said at last, "I'll give it a try. But if it doesn't work out don't blame me!"

Yocheved sighed with relief. "It will work out," she said triumphantly, "you'll see!"

They had reached the end of the lane by then and they both automatically turned back, as if, the mission accomplished, there was no point in going on walking. Spurred by her success, Yocheved decided to try and gain Nechy's confidence.

"Nechy," she said tentatively, "I wish you would tell me what's troubling you. We've been through so much together, I feel a bit like an older sister to you. You seem so different since you found your mother. Won't you let me know what's wrong?"

Nechy seemed to hesitate for a moment. Then she shook her head. "No, I can't!" she answered abruptly. "I wish you would all stop probing! You…and Shulamis…"

"We're not probing! We're your friends! We only want to

help you!" Yocheved protested.

Nechy stopped in her tracks and turned to face Yocheved, her face flushed. "Oh yes!" she cried, bitterness in her tone, "that's what you all say! You might even think it's true! But I know what you really think! I know you're all disgusted with me."

"Disgusted?" Yocheved stared at her, puzzled.

"Yes, you think I ought to be ashamed of myself behaving like that, when I'm really the lucky one! Everybody's thinking that— especially you and Chaya and Shulamis! Don't tell me you don't think that *you* would be different if it was your mother..."

Nechy broke off abruptly, overcome with remorse, as a look of pain crossed Yocheved's face. "Oh Yocheved!" she cried, bursting into tears, "I'm sorry! Oh, how could I?...Please, please forgive me...I'm so sorry!" Her words came out jerkily, amid sobs.

Yocheved put her arm comfortingly over the other girl's shoulder, but Nechy shook it off and pulled away.

"Don't!" she begged. "You're only making it worse! That's the whole trouble, don't you see? I can't face you all! I feel so absolutely guilty!" Turning away from Yocheved, Nechy ran up the lane, back toward school.

Yocheved stood and stared after Nechy running down the lane, gaping in astonishment. If only she understood what it all meant! She knew now that it was guilt that lay behind Nechy's peculiar behavior. But she couldn't understand what Nechy felt so guilty about.

Feeling deflated and utterly drained, Yocheved leaned against a tree. It was true that being close to Nechy and Shulamis *was* important. They were different from the other girls who had parents. Nechy's growing coldness was splitting up their little group. Suddenly, without warning, tears began to spill out of her eyes as a strange sadness overcame her. Taking off her glasses, she turned her face toward the tree, deriving a measure of comfort from the feel of its sturdy bark, and wept, something she had not done for a long time.

She was startled, some time later, by a man's voice behind her.

"Whatever is the matter?" the man demanded.

Wiping her eyes hurriedly with the back of her hand, Yocheved replaced her glasses hastily and swung round sharply to face the owner of the voice. She recognized him immediately as the new neighbor, although she had only seen him once and then he was clad in a formal suit and a bowler hat. Now he was wearing a knitted, sleeveless pullover over a checked shirt and his iron-grey hair was uncovered

Puffing at a pipe, he stood behind the wooden, rustic-style gate, regarding her quizzically from under his thick eyebrows. Beyond him, at the end of a winding path, Yocheved could see an ivy-covered cottage and she realized she was standing right outside Mr. Campbell's garden gate.

"Oh," she said quickly, feeling embarrassed. "I'm so sorry!"

"No need to apologize," he said, opening the gate and coming out. "You're in the street. It's a public thoroughfare. But in any case, why the tears? Is there something wrong?"

"N-no, nothing!" she assured him. "I'm just being stupid, that's all."

"You belong to that school there, don't you?" the man asked, jerking his head in the direction of Migdal Binoh. "I thought everyone was happy there."

"Oh we are!" Yocheved declared hastily. "It's just that I've had a silly quarrel with a friend."

"Well, you shouldn't let a little thing like that distress you so much," Mr. Campbell said patronizingly. "Your parents would be upset to know that you're unhappy."

"I have no parents," Yocheved informed him, wondering what on earth had made her tell him that. It was not something she normally talked about—let alone to a complete stranger! It must have been the whole conversation with Nechy that had thrown her off-balance.

Mr. Campbell tut-tutted and shook his head. "What happened to them?" he asked.

In spite of herself, Yocheved felt compelled to answer him. "They were killed," she said. "The Nazis shot them down!"

"Oh, how tragic! You poor girl!" Mr. Campbell exclaimed, but Yocheved had an uncanny feeling that the sympathy in his voice did not reach his eyes. But then, what could she expect of him? He had probably lived here in this country in relative security all through the war. How could *he* understand the horror of the atrocities that had taken place?

She had a sudden desire to get away as quickly as possible.

"Will you excuse me?" she said politely. "I must get back to school! Good afternoon…and thank you for your concern. Sorry if I disturbed you."

"Good afternoon, young lady," Mr. Campbell said, "and remember what I said. Don't let things get you down!"

Mr. Campbell then went inside his gate, but Yocheved had a feeling he was watching her as she hastened up the lane.

When Nechy returned on Monday morning from her weekend with her mother, the girls close to her scrutinized her searchingly, hoping to see her looking less tense. But the expression of strain and edginess was still there. Shulamis kept eyeing her with concern, but steered clear of any intimate conversation with her. Yocheved, still upset over Nechy's outburst, avoided any mention of the illustrations.

Yocheved was therefore immensely surprised when Nechy approached her a few days later, some sheets of drawing paper in her hand.

"I've done the drawings," Nechy said sullenly, thrusting the sheets at Yocheved. "But I don't know if you'll like them."

"Nechy! That's fantastic!" Yocheved cried, taking them from her with a smile of pleasure. "I knew you could do it!"

Nechy just shrugged and walked away.

Trying to ignore her feeling of irritation at Nechy's manner, Yocheved hurriedly sought out Frumie. She had not told Frumie about the disturbing brush she had had with Nechy—just that Nechy had said she would try to do the illustrations, which Frumie had looked upon as "quite an achievement!"

Now Yocheved proudly held the papers out to her. "Nechy's done them!" she announced triumphantly.

"Wow! That's terrific!" Frumie exclaimed. "Let's have a look at them."

Frumie's face fell as soon as she scanned the drawings. Yocheved too felt a sinking disappointment. The pictures, though artistically as good as ever, had a disturbing effect on the two girls.

"They're not her usual style," Frumie commented sadly.

"No, they're not," Yocheved agreed. "Look at those faces. They all look so... so...*angry*! Some of them look quite frightening! Frumie, what shall we do? We can't use these!"

"I know. But we can't *not* use them either. Who knows what effect that would have on Nechy!"

Yocheved was silent for a few moments, turning the matter over in her mind. Presently she said, "I think we'd better ask Suri. I know she said she was leaving it to us this time, but she's still in charge. She'll have to decide what to do."

Suri Bernstein was as uncertain as they were. "It's a problem," she admitted. "We don't want to upset Nechy—specially the way she is at the moment. But we can't possibly print these. They're positively scary! I wonder what's got into her!"

"Maybe we should speak to Mrs. Langfeld," Frumie suggested.

"No, I don't think we should bother Mrs. Langfeld with it," Suri said. "She's got enough on her plate. We'll have to work out a solution, somehow."

Yocheved gave a deep sigh. "I guess there's nothing else to do," she said, somewhat reluctantly. "The magazine has to get done. We need those drawings! I will have to speak to Nechy and ask her to alter them a bit. Though I'm not looking forward to it, I can tell you!"

She found Nechy alone in the classroom later that afternoon and took the opportunity to tackle her. Nechy's reaction was not unexpected and Yocheved could not help wishing it had not been her task to be the cause of it.

Her eyes flashing, Nechy snatched the pictures out of her hand, "I told you that you wouldn't like them!" she cried. "Why did you talk me into doing them? I didn't want to! You made me feel bad for letting you down, so I tried. But that's all I can do and if they're no use, I can't help it!" And before Yocheved could stop her she tore the papers up, throwing the fragments onto the floor and running out of the room.

With a heavy heart, Yocheved bent down to gather up the pieces, screwing them up into a ball and throwing them into the waste-paper basket. Oh, what had she done? She had meant well. How had it misfired so badly? Now Nechy would be more unhappy than ever. If only she had left things well alone!

It was just too bad about the illustrations. She would ask Judy Kleiner to do one or two more and the magazine would just have less illustrations, that was all. Why, oh why, she asked herself, couldn't they have decided to do that in the first place?

ANOTHER HURDLE

RS. LANGFELD, HAVING FINISHED WRITING her two weekly letters to her children, placed them in the appropriate envelopes. The letter to her son, Nochum Tzvi and his wife, Gita was not very long because she had had a fairly uneventful week at school and thus could not find much to write. She had already told them in previous letters about the new neighbors, complete with descriptions, and about the two awkward hurdles she had come up against, namely the inspector's visit and the interview with Mr. Dobson. The letter she had written now was filled mainly with inquiries about friends and acquaintances in London as well as questions about their little son, Moishy, whom she missed terribly and to whom she sent an abundance of love and kisses!

To her seventeen-year-old daughter, Bayla, a student at Gateshead Seminary, she wrote of her concern for Nechy, whose changed nature continued to baffle her. Bayla knew the four refugee girls well, as her mother had often invited them to her house when they had lived in London, and Mrs. Langfeld knew she would understand her frustration even though she could not do much to help from so far away.

'I've tried talking to Nechy,' she wrote, 'but I didn't make much headway. She seems to have closed up completely. All that came over was her feeling of guilt—though I don't know what for—and her regret at the way she was treating Shulamis and Yocheved, her closest friends....'

Sticking stamps onto the two envelopes, Mrs. Langfeld slipped on her jacket and went out of the office, making her way out to the mailbox, just outside the school gates.

She had just reached it when she saw Mr. Campbell coming up the lane toward her.

Throwing the letters in hastily, she tried to hurry back into the school grounds, but it was no use. Mr. Campbell was gesticulating, making it obvious that he wanted to speak to her and it would have been extremely rude to ignore him.

With a little sigh of impatience, she stood waiting until he reached her.

"Good afternoon, Mr. Campbell," she said, sounding more friendly than she felt.

"Good afternoon, Mrs. Langfeld," he said affably, raising his hat.

"Quite warm for late October, isn't it?"

"Yes, it is," Mrs. Langfeld agreed, wishing she had chosen a different time to post her letters. She had far more important things to do than stand around discussing the weather!

"I must congratulate you," Mr. Campbell said. "I hear the school inspector was most impressed by your school's high standards!"

"How did you know that?" the headmistress stared at him in surprise.

"Aha!" he said teasingly, "a little bird told me!" He threw

back his head and laughed, enjoying his little joke. However, seeing Mrs. Langfeld's puzzled expression, he sobered down. "Actually," he explained, "it was Horace Dobson who told me."

"You know Mr. Dobson?" Mrs. Langfeld continued to look astonished.

"Oh yes! We belong to the same golf club. I play golf with him every Sunday afternoon."

So it could well have been Mr. Campbell who had imparted the information about her lack of qualifications after all! In fact Mrs. Langfeld was now quite convinced that it was! She was tempted to ask him about it, but decided not to. Better not bring up the subject again. Let sleeping dogs lie, she told herself.

Not wishing to carry on the conversation, she took a step toward the school gate, but Mr. Campbell held up his thick hand as if to stop her going in.

"Mrs. Langfeld," he said, "there is something I have wanted to ask you ever since I heard about your good results—or rather, my wife asked me to ask you. You see, Emily's sister, who lives in Devon, has a daughter of thirteen and she's thinking of sending her to boarding school."

Oh no! Mrs. Langfeld thought, knowing only too well what was coming.

"Emily thought it would be so nice if she could go to your school. 'Just imagine,' she said to me, 'having Lucinda right next door! And at such a good school too!' It would be so good for my wife, Mrs. Langfeld…"

"Just a minute, Mr. Campbell," Mrs. Langfeld interrupted him, "I think I've already told you that we don't accept non-Jewish pupils!"

"Yes, you did. But I'm sure just one wouldn't matter!"

"I'm afraid we can't make any exceptions," the headmistress said firmly.

"But I can't see why…" Mr. Campbell began, plaintively, his bushy eyebrows raised in surprise.

"It's too complicated to explain," Mrs. Langfeld replied, "and there is no point in discussing this further. Good day, Mr. Campbell, and please tell your wife I am sorry I can't oblige!"

"I'm sure you're making a big mistake!" Mr. Campbell called after her as she walked away.

The conversation had quite unnerved Mrs. Langfeld. He had looked so angry as she had turned her back on him and it had made her feel embarrassed. She had not wanted to hurt his feelings, but how could she have explained to him why she had to reject his niece? All the same, she reflected, he could not be as anti-Semitic as she had originally thought if he was willing to have a relative enrolled in a Jewish school!

She hoped she had made her position clear and that the matter would end there, but she had an uneasy feeling that he would not let it rest so easily. He seemed to be an extremely persistent person.

However, the pressure came eventually from a different source altogether.

It started with a telephone call a few days after her meeting with Mr. Campbell.

"Mrs…er…Langfeld?" a very affected female voice came over the line. "My name is Lady Harrington. My husband is Sir Rudolph Harrington, the well-known historian."

"Oh, yes?" Mrs. Langfeld had heard of him and wondered what was coming.

"Mrs. Langfeld," Lady Harrington gushed. "I've heard such *wonderful* things about your school! And I've decided it's *just* the place for my Felicity! You cannot imagine how *glad* I was to hear that there is such an *exclusive* boarding school right on my doorstep, so to speak! We live in High Wycombe, and it will be so nice to know that even though Felicity is at boarding school she is still not far away! She's an only child, you see…"

Mrs. Langfeld decided it was high time she interrupted this garrulous rigmarole. "Lady Harrington," she said firmly, "before you carry on let me tell you that it will not be possible for me to accept your daughter."

There was a stunned silence at the other end of the line before Lady Harrington exclaimed, in a tone expressing shock and incredulity, "What was that you said? You won't accept her? But that's ridiculous! You don't even know…"

"Please let me explain," Mrs. Langfeld cut in again quickly, "the reason I cannot accept her is because this is a Jewish school."

"Oh, is that all?" there was a note of relief in the woman's voice. "Well that doesn't bother me! We don't have any particular religion ourselves, so I don't mind what kind of school she goes to as long as she gets a good all round education. She doesn't have to take part in your religious assemblies—or whatever you have—but it doesn't matter if she does. I'm all for her broadening her outlook…"

Mrs. Langfeld sighed with exasperation. This was going to be a difficult person to put off! She would have to be short and sharp with her. "I'm afraid there's more to it than that," she said, "but it would take too long to explain. The fact is that we only have religious Jewish girls here—*and no one else*! I cannot make any exceptions!"

"I see!" Lady Harrington's tone was icy. "And that is your last word?"

"Yes, it is!" the headmistress replied resolutely.

"Well I think it's quite preposterous!" the woman exploded. "This is the only boarding school in Buckinghamshire and you have no right to adopt this 'dog-in-the-manger' attitude! I shall complain to the local education authorities about this. We'll see what *they* have to say about it!"

"Yes, do that!" Mrs. Langfeld retorted, but she realized she wasn't speaking to anyone, as Lady Harrington, with a curt "good day!" had slammed the receiver down.

Somewhat shaken, Mrs. Langfeld sat and reflected over the situation. She was not unduly worried, as she knew she was within her rights. This was a private, self-supporting school and she could pick and choose which girls to accept— or refuse. But it was unpleasant, nevertheless, to be the object of a complaint. She hoped the authorities would support her and put Lady Harrington in her place!

Although she heard no more from the historian's wife, that was not the end of the affair. Similar incidents occurred with alarming rapidity. Mrs. Langfeld became inundated with telephone calls from people, mostly fairly local, who wanted to enroll girls in her school.

There was a prominent surgeon from Aylesbury who wanted to send his daughter; a politician with twins; a solicitor from nearby Dunstable; a few farmers and even the mayor of Elmsleigh, who begged her to accept his granddaughter. One or two understood the position, but most were angry at her refusal.

The culmination of this annoying episode came in the form of a telephone call from an irate Mr. Dobson.

"Mrs. Langfeld!" he growled, "what do you think you're playing at?"

"Playing at? I beg your pardon! I don't understand!"

"Don't you?" he said gruffly. "Here we are, trying to promote your school and help it grow and all you're doing is turning down applicants! I'd like to know why!"

"Because this is a school for religious Jewish girls only," Mrs. Langfeld replied simply.

"I fail to understand the sense in that," Mr. Dobson complained.

"We've been bogged down with complaints about it—from some very influential people too! People round here don't like it, I can tell you!"

Patiently Mrs. Langfeld tried to explain that religious Jews have a particular way of life which had to be adhered to all the time and it was therefore impossible to absorb outsiders into the school. She had a feeling that Mr. Dobson was, at last, grasping the situation, though he was reluctant to admit it.

"I don't know," he said, his tone still dubious, "I still think it's not advisable for your pupils to be so severely segregated. They should learn to mix and become integrated in our society."

Mrs. Langfeld decided not to pursue the subject. How could she expect him to understand? Orthodox Judaism was complex to outsiders, and because of his negative attitude she was finding it difficult to easily explain it to him. Instead Mrs. Langfeld pressed on with her argument, justifying her action.

"I'm sure I am within my rights," she insisted. "This is a private school, completely self-supporting, and I don't think I can be forced to accept pupils against my will. Is that not so?"

"Legally, yes," Mr. Dobson agreed. "But I think you should know that you were on the top priority list for a grant to extend and refurbish your building...as well as being considered for aid concerning books and equipment. I'm afraid you will forfeit those benefits if you persist with your ideas."

"Mr. Dobson," Mrs. Langfeld replied with dignity. "We managed perfectly well without these things till now, and I daresay we will continue to manage. We have the generous support of Sir Isaac Greenhorn, as well as a committee in London, which organizes fund-raising functions and collects money on our behalf. So I shall continue to stick to my principles!"

Mr. Dobson murmured something about wishing her luck and hung up, leaving Mrs. Langfeld in a thoughtful frame of mind.

How had this strange state of affairs come about? It had obviously been instigated by Mr. Campbell. For a moment, she felt quite sorry for the Campbells. They seemed so desperate to have Mrs. Campbell's niece at the school that they went to such lengths to bring it about.

She thought with nostalgia of old Mr. Butterworth, always greeting her or the girls with a friendly word, but, in general, he quietly minded his own business. The only time he made his presence felt was when he occasionally brought in a bunch of flowers from his carefully tended garden, to "brighten the place up" as he put it.

Her fleeting moment of pity for the Campbells was soon replaced by anger. Perhaps they really meant well—she didn't know—but they seemed to be continually making trouble for the school!

She decided to avoid them as much as she could from now on, hoping she would not encounter them in the lane, as it was becoming extremely difficult to be cordial to them!

PLANS AND
COUNTER-PLANS

"**S**hulamis?" There was a hesitant note in Nechy's voice as she addressed her friend, "there's something I'd like to ask you...but you can say 'no' if you want..."

Shulamis turned toward Nechy, an expression of eagerness on her face. Nechy was wearing a bright rose-colored headband which made her look happier than she'd been for a while. And her wool school uniform looked neater than it had been lately. Nechy's approach, however tentative, was the very first hint of a drop in the coldness that had developed between them and she was sure of one thing. Whatever Nechy's request, there was no way she would refuse it!

"Ask away!" she said encouragingly.

"Well...you see...i-it's about the holidays..." Nechy seemed uncomfortable as she shifted from one foot to another and lowered her head. "You know I'm going to spend it with my mother, at the nursing home in Chingford...well, the matron said I could bring a friend with me—she said it would be advisable—so I thought…well…I wondered if you would you be interested in coming?" Nechy's obvious embarrassment caused the last few words to come out almost as a whisper.

The warm feeling that had enveloped Shulamis fell a few degrees. Oh Nechy, she thought with disappointment, why didn't you ask me earlier? Only two days ago she had received an exciting invitation which she had accepted. Simi Korwich had come up to her looking starry-eyed, with a letter in her hand.

"Shulamis, I've just got a letter from my mother and I'm all excited. You see, we've been having a loft built in our house and the workmen have just finished it. I'm going to have my own bedroom in it and the rest has been made into a big play-room, with a ping-pong table and room for all sorts of games! Mummy says I should invite a friend to spend the holidays with me. Will you come? *Please* say yes! It'll be loads of fun!"

Naturally Shulamis had agreed to come. Although she had had a few other invitations, Simi's invitation had seemed the most attractive. Besides, she knew she would be doing Simi a favor too. Living in Golders Green, Simi was a little cut off from the other girls during the holidays since all the other girls seemed to live near one another. But since the extension had been built, there was room for her to have some company. It all sounded like a lot of fun and Shulamis had been looking forward to it.

And now, here she was, faced with Nechy's request, which she knew she could not turn down! What in the world was she going to do?

It did not take more than a minute for her mind to clear. It was quite obvious really. Never mind her disappointment and the feeling that she was letting Simi down. Nechy needed her and her need was the greatest! And the old bond between the refugee girls was still powerful. Hoping her friend had not detected any sign of hesitation on her part, she gave her a bright smile and said, "Of course, Nechy! I'd love to come!

Nechy's face expressed relief and gratitude as she eyed Shulamis searchingly. "Are you sure?" she asked, somewhat skeptically. "I know it's not exactly the most cheerful place to be in. Some of the people there are quite ill and most of them are not in the happiest frame of mind. And Mummy..." her voice trailed off and her face clouded over, "...well, it's no use talking about it now," she said solemnly, "you'll see for yourself, I expect."

It was the nearest to confiding in her that Nechy was likely to come, Shulamis realized, and now was not the time to probe further. At the moment, Nechy just needed reassurance.

Shulamis grabbed Nechy's hand. "You'll be there, won't you," she said warmly, "that's good enough company for me!"

There was a depth of feeling in Nechy's eyes as she looked at her friend. "Thanks, Shulamis," she said solemnly, "you're really a friend! I don't know what I'd have done if I'd have had to spend two weeks there on my own...," her voice trailed off and the familiar guilty look crept over her face. Obviously feeling she had said too much, she squeezed Shulamis's hand and quickly walked away.

Shulamis, left staring after Nechy, was more convinced than ever that she had made the right decision. But now she had to figure out what she was going to tell Simi. How could she make her understand what had prompted her to change her mind at the last minute?

Simi, the daughter of rather indulgent parents who rarely refused her anything, did not understand at all and expressed her disappointment in no uncertain terms.

"I don't know how you can prefer a place like that!" she

protested, shaking her long, straight hair. "It'll be awfully dreary! And anyway, it's not fair! I asked you first! I've already written to my mother to say that you're coming."

"I'm sorry Simi, really I am! Can't you ask someone else?"

"You know very well I can't," Simi replied in a disgruntled tone, "all the girls are looking forward to going home. No one's seen their parents since after *Yom Tov*."

"What about Yocheved and Chaya?" Shulamis suggested a little impatiently.

"Well, I could ask them, I suppose, but I think I heard Yocheved tell someone they've been invited. Oh, Shulamis! Please change your mind! I'll explain to Nechy that I really asked you first…"

"No!" Shulamis cried. "I don't want Nechy to know anything at all about this! Do you hear?"

"Okay, okay! I won't tell her!" Simi declared. "Though I don't know what *you're* so worked up about. I'm the one who should be shouting! You've absolutely *ruined* my holiday!"

Shulamis apologized again, telling herself that she would make amends by thinking of an alternative solution for Simi. But days went by and nothing came to mind.

By now December had arrived, throwing the school into an atmosphere of frenzied activity. Besides end-of-term exams there was Chanukah to organize and preparations for various social events were soon well under way. Shulamis, finding herself caught up in the hustle and bustle, gave the problem of Simi little thought.

One thing did strike her though, and she wondered at first if she might be imagining it. Nechy seemed to be avoiding her. However, when she did manage to get Nechy on her own it was all too obvious. The coldness between them had returned, more noticeably than ever before.

"Tell me about Chingford," she said, hoping the reminder

of the forthcoming holiday would warm up her friend's attitude once more.

"Why do you want to know?" Nechy asked curtly.

"Well, I am coming there with you, aren't I? So I…"

"I'd rather you weren't!" Nechy snapped. Shulamis stared at her, open-mouthed. "B-but Nechy?" she stammered, "I-I don't understand! You asked me…"

"I know I did," Nechy said. "But I didn't mean for you to make such a sacrifice! I don't need that, thank you very much!"

"Sacrifice? I don't know what you mean! I want to come with you! I was looking forward to it!"

"Oh come on, Shulamis, don't pretend! You can't possibly prefer that to going to Simi Korwich's house."

"H-how do you know about that?" Shulamis blurted out, dumb-founded. "I told Simi not to tell you!"

"So it *is* true!" Nechy cried, almost triumphantly. "I overheard Simi telling Yocheved that you really wanted to go with her but that you felt you ought to come with me. Well, *I* don't want you to, so you can go with Simi…and enjoy yourself!"

And before Shulamis could utter a word, Nechy had walked away.

Shulamis felt as if the ground had slipped away from underneath her. Why, oh why did Nechy have to overhear Simi's words? Couldn't Simi have been more careful? She knew she couldn't really blame Simi, but she was sure of one thing. Even if she didn't go with Nechy she would *not* change her mind about going to Golders Green. If she did, she would surely lose Nechy's friendship forever.

Suddenly Shulamis felt completely drained. She had tried so hard to do the right thing with Nechy. All this was too much for her. She leaned against the wall and sighed deeply.

Etty walked by just then, and hearing the heavy sigh, turned round sharply.

"Shulamis! Are you all right? You look awfully upset!"

Overcome with an urge to discuss her predicament with someone, Shulamis poured out the whole story to Etty.

"I feel so bad about both of them!" Shulamis said, almost in tears. "It's going to take me all my time to persuade Nechy that I really want to go with her—if I ever manage to do this!—and I know I ought to think of someone who would go to Simi's...Hey!" she exclaimed as a thought struck her, "what about you? Wouldn't you like to go? After all, you see your mother the whole time you're in school. Maybe it would be nice to go away for a change!"

"Wait a minute," Etty cried, "I can't just go up to Simi and say 'I'd like to come to your house for the holidays.' How do you know she would want me to?"

"But if she asked you," Shulamis persisted, "would you accept?"

"I might. If Mummy doesn't mind."

Shulamis said no more but hurried off to seek out Simi and make her suggestion. "I'll ask her, but I can't imagine that she'll come," Simi commented sulkily, treating Shulamis to a look of exasperation before turning away. Not waiting to find out the outcome of her idea, she then went to search for Nechy. She had done her duty as far as Simi was concerned, she told herself, but Nechy was going to be a harder nut to crack. And crack it she must!

She found Nechy alone in the classroom, where she had come to replace some books in her desk. As soon as Nechy saw her, she began to make for the door, but Shulamis reached it first and stood firmly in front of it, barring the other girl's exit.

"Let me go out!" Nechy cried angrily.

"No!" Shulamis declared, her face red and determined. "Not until you've listened to me!"

Nechy's lip began to tremble, but she bit it hard and shook her head, her hair falling in front of her face.

"Nechy, please!" Shulamis begged. "I understand how you feel, but believe me, you've got it all wrong! However upset you are, you at least *owe* it to me to listen to my explanation!"

Nechy's shoulders drooped as her resistance wavered. "Okay," she said resignedly, "say what you must. But it won't make any difference! I know you mean well, but please don't be a martyr for my sake! I don't need you to sacrifice your time off for me!"

"It's not like that!" Shulamis protested, running a hand through her dark curls, an almost pleading expression in her clear brown eyes. "Look, please let's sit down and I'll explain." She sat herself down at a desk near the door and Nechy followed suit a little distance away, clenching her fists and biting her lip to stop its quivering.

"Before you even asked me to join you I knew you were going to Chingford," Shulamis went on, "but I would never have dreamt of asking if I could come with you. I wouldn't have wanted to intrude—you had pushed me away and so I was staying away!" Nechy opened her mouth to say something, but Shulamis ignored her and forged on. "If only you'd asked me earlier! As it was, Simi invited me and I accepted. Where else should I have gone? I haven't got a home or any parents or relatives to go to, you know!" She was aware of a softening in Nechy's expression. "...And then you came along with your invitation and *of course* I decided to drop the other one! I was so thrilled that you'd asked me after the way things have been between us lately! I've been longing to get close to you again...like we were before. Don't you remember? You said we were like sisters!"

Shulamis broke off as, her own eyes brimming with tears, she noticed tears coursing unchecked down Nechy's cheeks.

"Oh, Nechy!" she cried, getting up from her seat and sitting down at the desk in front of Nechy. "I'm sorry! I never, ever meant to hurt you!" She leaned forward, toward her friend, and gazed into her eyes.

"*You* hurt *me?*" Nechy exclaimed, amid sobs, "it's the other way round! I'm the one who's been doing the hurting! I don't know why you even bother with me! I'm behaving like an absolute pest."

"No, you're not!" Shulamis contradicted her, "you're just all mixed up—and I wish I could help you!"

"You can't!" Nechy declared. "*No one* can! I don't even understand it myself!" And Nechy lowered her head and lapsed into silence for a few moments. Shulamis, not sure what to say, watched her quietly. "Shulamis," Nechy said presently, lifting her head and pushing her hair out of her eyes, "when we're at the nursing home you might see...and hear...some upsetting things..." she stopped and eyed her friend searchingly, "that is, if you still want to come..."

"Of course I do!" Shulamis reassured her.

The school bell rang out shrilly, making both girls jump. Shulamis stood up hastily, wiping her eyes with the back of her hand. "The others will be here for lessons in a minute. We'll pretend we've been studying for the French exam." She made her way to her own desk, with Nechy following her example. "Let's not speak about this any more for the time being. We'll have plenty of time to talk when we're at Chingford!"

MEETING
MRS. HOROWITZ

SHULAMIS AWOKE WITH A START, CONVINCED that the screams she had heard were part of her nightmare. Her surroundings seemed strangely unfamiliar and the part of her brain that was fully awake concluded that she was not in the dormitory at school. But where…? Of course! She remembered now…, she was at the nursing home in Chingford! And she could still hear the screams!

The room was not in total darkness, as a small panel of clear glass at the top of the door let in a shaft of light from the corridor. Shulamis could see Nechy standing by her bed, putting on her pink dressing-gown and stepping into her fluffy slippers.

"Nechy?" she whispered questioningly.

"Shh!" Nechy whispered back, "go back to sleep. It's Mummy. I must go to her!" Nechy then tiptoed out of the room, closing the door firmly behind her.

Perhaps I should go with her, Shulamis thought, but,

afraid she would be trespassing on their privacy, she remained where she was. However, she could not go to back to sleep and she lay in bed, listening apprehensively. The screaming seemed to come to an abrupt halt and Shulamis pictured Nechy putting a comforting arm round her mother and speaking soothingly to her. Other footsteps could be heard hurrying past the door...obviously one of the night nurses going to deal with the situation. She would probably give Mrs. Horowitz a sedative to calm her down, Shulamis imagined. But poor Nechy! What a burden she carried on her shoulders!

Reflecting on the last two days—since she and Nechy had come to Chingford—Shulamis found she was beginning to understand Nechy's problem. What she couldn't understand was why Nechy had shut herself inward, refusing to talk about it.

Her mind went back to the moment she had first set eyes on Mrs. Horowitz. Shulamis and Nechy had arrived at the nursing home early in the afternoon and Nechy had first taken her to the matron's office to introduce her. Then they had taken their suitcases upstairs to their small room. It was as if Nechy was reluctant to take her friend to meet her mother and was pushing off the moment.

When at last the time came, and Shulamis followed Nechy along the corridor to Mrs. Horowitz's room, she was apprehensive, not knowing what to expect. As they entered the room it seemed at first as if there was no one in it. Then Shulamis became aware of movement coming from a white wicker chair near the bed, as a figure arose from it and came toward them.

Shulamis took in the woman's appearance with a sense of shock. So this was Nechy's mother! How pale and thin she looked!

A faded floral headscarf framed her gaunt face and her deep-set brown eyes reflected the horrors she had suffered. She walked with a slight stoop, which made her appear shorter than her actual height.

Mrs. Horowitz greeted them with a wan smile, and held her arms out to Nechy, who ran over to her at once. Shulamis felt very moved as she watched mother and daughter hug each other.

Conversation, Shulamis recalled, had been exceedingly difficult; Nechy struggled to speak Yiddish, dotting her sentences with many English words, which seemed to make her mother wince. Shulamis managed to make herself understood with the few German words she still remembered from her early years. It was Mrs. Horowitz herself who kept the talk going, speaking fluently in Yiddish, which the girls were fortunately able to follow. Although her manner was generally languid and lethargic, there were moments when her speech was more animated, giving Shulamis a glimpse of the person she had once been, before the Nazis had reduced her to this weak, apathetic state.

Now that she had met Mrs. Horowitz, Shulamis half expected Nechy to open up and unburden herself, but as they prepared to retire for the night, she soon realized that no confidence was forthcoming. Nechy talked about everything but her problem. All the same, the picture was becoming clearer to Shulamis. She felt she was beginning to understand the cause of Nechy's distress. Nechy was, after all, still so young and needed to be cared for herself. When her mother had so miraculously appeared, she must have imagined that things would be as they were before, with Mrs. Horowitz looking after her as any normal mother would. Instead, it was Nechy who had to do the caring, and although she was surely happy to do whatever she could for her mother, it was a burden that sat heavily on Nechy's young shoulders. Knowing how much more fortunate she was than her three orphaned friends, she was obviously riddled with guilt for resenting that burden. Poor Nechy! Shulamis longed to put her friend's mind at rest and ease her sense of guilt, but how could she if Nechy did not talk to her about her feelings?

"I hope it doesn't rain tomorrow," Nechy was saying. "When I come here I usually take Mummy out for a walk, so I thought we'd go to Epping Forest. It's quite near here. Do you remember Epping Forest?" she asked. "We once went there for a *Lag B'omer* outing."

"Yes, I remember," Shulamis said, "though it was years ago. I'd love to see it again. It was lovely."

The weather, the next day, was on their side. Although cold, the sky was bright blue and it was sunny. Immediately after lunch, the two girls and Mrs. Horowitz wrapped up warmly and set out.

It took them quite a long time to get to the forest as Mrs. Horowitz, still weak, had to sit down and rest on every bench they came across. When they arrived at last, Shulamis just stood still for a moment, taking in the sight. Even in the winter the forest was beautiful! In spite of the bleak bareness of the trees, there was a dignified splendor about the place.

They walked into the forest and found a bench to sit down. Shulamis took a deep breath and looked around her.

"Isn't it tranquil and relaxing here," she commented.

"Yes, it is," Nechy agreed. "Oh look, there's a squirrel!" They sat in companionable silence for while, watching the squirrel scurry up a tree and jump from branch to branch. Then Shulamis said, "Nechy, why didn't you bring your sketch pad? You ought to get this beautiful scenery down on paper!"

Nechy just shrugged and Shulamis, unaware that she had

touched a sore spot, turned to Mrs. Horowitz and said, "Nechy draws very well." Then, seeing the blank look on the woman's face, she repeated in German, "*Nechy zeichnet sehr gut.*"

Mrs. Horowitz's eyes lit up as she nodded in agreement, informing her that, even as a small child, Nechy had shown talent.

Shulamis thought Nechy's heightened color was due to embarrassment at being discussed, but as the afternoon wore on and they made their way back to the nursing home, she realized that her friend had become quiet and withdrawn.

In their room that night the atmosphere was strained. Shulamis could feel that the barrier had come between them once more. What had happened? Was it something she had said? She strained her mind, trying to remember, convinced that if she couldn't figure it out she would not sleep a wink. But the afternoon's outing and the bracing air had made her tired and soon she dozed off.

And now, having been awakened by the screams, she found sleep evading her after all. As she lay thinking of all that had transpired during the last two days, it came to her quite clearly. Nechy's reticence had definitely begun after the mention of her artistic abilities. She was still brooding over the matter, wondering how to make amends, when Nechy returned.

Not sure what to say to her, she kept very still, pretending to be asleep, but watching Nechy nevertheless, through half-closed eyes. She saw her shrug off her dressing-gown and kick off her slippers, giving a deep sigh as she sat down at the edge of her bed, a sad and forlorn figure.

"Nechy..." she said, feeling suddenly that she had to speak to her, "are you all right?"

In reply, Nechy burst into tears and flung herself face downwards onto the bed, sobbing into her pillow. Shulamis went across to her immediately and, sitting down on the bed, she put her arm across the girl's shaking shoulders, letting her cry. When, at last, Nechy's weeping ceased, Shulamis said, "Nechy...you have *got* to talk to me! If you don't share your burden with someone you'll make yourself ill. And what good will you be to your mother then?"

Nechy turned a tear-stained face toward her. "I'm no good to her now either!" she declared. "If I was a bit stronger I'd stay with her all the time—not keep running away! She relies on me. I'm all she's got left in the world!"

"If you call coming to school 'running away,' " Shulamis said, "that's silly. You can't just miss out on your schooling, and your mother doesn't really want you to."

"I know," Nechy said, a rueful note in her voice, "she keeps saying she doesn't want to be a burden on me. She tells me so many times how much she wants to be a good mother and look after me. Sometimes she seems so much better that I think it's really going to happen. And then she has these nightmares and she seems to go right back again! That's why I feel so guilty. It's because I'm glad to return to school...especially when things get difficult. You don't know what it's like sometimes." There was a note of desperation in her voice.

"Nechy, tell me about it," Shulamis prompted softly. She went across to her own bed, took off her blanket and, wrapping it round her, sat down again on the end of Nechy's bed.

Nechy, sitting up and drawing her blanket up to her shoulders, began to speak in a low voice. "Do you remember how excited I was when Mummy came back? Of course I was shocked by her appearance...just looking at her was painful for me...but I thought everything was going to be wonderful! I only wanted to be with her and I didn't dream I would ever *want* to leave her side. Only it didn't turn out quite like I expected." Her voice shook and she paused.

"Because of the language problem?" Shulamis asked.

"Partly," Nechy replied. "But I guess I would have managed somehow. No, it was because Mummy wouldn't come back to the present. She just went on reliving the terrible things she had been through. She kept on telling me about them and sometimes I just couldn't bear it! Shulamis, you just can't imagine!" She broke off, crying and covering her face with her hands and shaking her head, as if trying to throw off the memories. Presently she continued. "And the screaming that you heard tonight...well, at first that went on every night."

"So she does seem to be getting better," Shulamis commented, glad to find words of encouragement.

"Y-yes..." Nechy admitted, "but I don't think she will ever get those nightmares out of her system. You should see what she's like! She looks so frightened, she gets so hysterical, and I can't even help properly! I'm just a kid! And she doesn't understand half of what I say!"

"Has she tried to learn a bit of English?" Shulamis mused.

"She doesn't seem to want to," Nechy said. "It's funny, but she becomes sort of agitated whenever I speak English. I wonder why?" Nechy sat quietly for a while, looking pensive. Unable to suggest a possible explanation, Shulamis searched for something to say. "What do the doctors say about her?" she asked. "Have you spoken to anyone about it?"

"Yes, I spoke to Mrs. Laufer...you know, the matron. She did say they are a bit worried because her progress is so slow," Nechy sighed deeply. "I'm also worried! I wish she'd get better already, and be more like her old self. You don't know what she used to be like! She was always cheerful and quite busy. She'd cook up a storm. Our house was usually bustling with guests and nothing was too much for her!" Obviously basking in the memory, Nechy lapsed into another silence.

Shulamis said nothing—what was there for her to say?—and presently Nechy went on. "Mrs. Laufer says they think that once her state of mind improves she's sure to get better physically. They've got a doctor coming tomorrow—a psychiatrist. She's Czech, so she'll be able to speak to her. Perhaps they'll let me have a word with her after she's seen Mummy. I hope this will help her at last!" she added on a desperate note.

"Oh, I hope so!" Shulamis echoed.

The two girls sat without speaking for a while. Then Shulamis broke the silence.

"Nechy…" she began with feeling, "thank you for telling me all this. I've been absolutely puzzled by the way you were behaving—at least I understand now. But Nechy, why did you keep it all to yourself for so long? Why didn't you talk to me? After all, we've been friends forever! We're closer than sisters! We're best friends! I mean, what are friends for if you can't turn to them when you need them?"

"I don't know," Nechy looked down, unable to meet her friend's eyes. "You were so happy for me…everybody was. How could I return to school, moaning and complaining? I felt so guilty even to be thinking that way—and if I disapproved of my reaction, how could I expect you not to disapprove of me? It's just so complicated!"

"But I wouldn't have!" Shulamis began, protesting.

"You would!" Nechy insisted. "You would have thought I was exaggerating the situation—that I should be glad to have my mother back…which I am, all the same! You would have told me not to go to pieces because things were a bit difficult. And you'd have been right. I truly ought to be able to cope!"

"Nechy, *stop* feeling guilty! I think you're coping extremely well, considering. You are just a teenager, after all! But you'll do even better if you stop shutting out your friends. We all want to help you!"

In spite of herself, Nechy smiled. "Thanks, Shulamis. You've no idea how much you've helped me tonight. And I won't shut you out anymore! As long as you understand that I've changed and I really can't be as lighthearted and carefree as I used to be."

"Oh, Nechy, you will be lighthearted again one day!" Shulamis insisted. "Once your mother is better, I'm sure a weight will lift off your shoulders."

"Maybe," Nechy looked at Shulamis skeptically. "Now I think we'd better both try to get some sleep, even though there's not much left of the night! There's a busy day ahead tomorrow and I want to be alert for it!"

DR. SYKORA

T HE TRAIN JOSTLED ALONG JERKILY, MAKING frequent stops at various small stations with unfamiliar names. Shulamis sat in her seat with an open book on her lap, but she found herself unable to concentrate. When she wasn't peering anxiously out of the window—to make sure she wouldn't miss the Chingford stop—her eyes would stray upwards toward the luggage rack above her head, where she could see the brown paper parcel resting beneath her coat. Had she done the right thing? she wondered. How would Nechy react when she unwrapped the parcel and saw the contents? Nechy had become so moody. It was hard to tell what her reaction would be! Would she withdraw into her shell again? For a moment Shulamis was overcome with misgivings. What was she thinking of, jeopardizing their newly reestablished closeness? It was probably better that she not give Nechy the parcel after all. But no, she convinced herself a few moments later, that was defeatist. After all, Shulamis reasoned, her natural kind-heartedness and the impulsive streak in her nature taking over, it might just give Nechy the push she needed, in which case it was well worth the risk.

The train stopped briefly at another station and Shulamis realized that Chingford was the next stop. Climbing up and taking down her things, she shrugged into her coat and made her way to the door of the carriage, where she stood waiting, ready to alight as soon as the train stopped. Normally she would have enjoyed the lovely country scenery they were passing through, but today she hardly took it in. Her mind was on Nechy and the Czech doctor who had come to see Mrs. Horowitz. She wondered how they had fared.

Not wanting to be in the way, she had told Nechy that she would leave the nursing home while the doctor was seeing Nechy's mother and she'd spend the morning in London.

"Oh, you don't have to go away!" Nechy had protested.

"Well, I'd like to do a bit of shopping," Shulamis had said, a plan suddenly forming in her mind. It had seemed a good idea at the time and she had been so carried away with it that she hadn't stopped to think of the possible repercussions it might have. That is, until now, when she was on her way back to Chingford.

The train rumbled into the station and ground to a noisy halt. A cold, blustery wind was blowing and Shulamis pulled her wool collar up round her ears as she made her way along the winding lanes to the nursing home. As she approached the building, she could see a woman walking down the path, carrying a black attaché case. She reached the large, wrought-iron gates just as the woman was pulling them open. Shulamis regarded the woman with interest. Quite tall and slender, she wore a brown coat with a large fur collar. A hat made of the same fur was perched on top of her dark, frizzy hair that was streaked with gray. Her face, though not particularly striking and largely taken up with a pair of round, tortoiseshell-rimmed spectacles, looked intelligent and kind and her whole bearing was dignified. She smiled at Shulamis when she saw her and to Shulamis's surprise she stopped and extended a leather gloved hand.

"You must be Nechy's friend," she spoke with a warm, rich voice and an accent Shulamis did not recognize. "I am Dr. Sykora," she went on, seeing the girl's puzzled expression. "I've just been to see Mrs. Horowitz."

"Oh yes!" Shulamis's face cleared and she grasped the woman's hand.

"I'm so glad Nechy has you here," Dr. Sykora said. "She's told me what a good friend you are! And believe me, that is something she really needs at the moment!"

Shulamis blushed, but there was concern in her voice. "Oh please," she said anxiously, "tell me how I can help her!"

"Just by giving her support," the doctor replied. "She has quite a burden on her shoulders for someone so young!"

"I know...and I'll do my best." Shulamis sighed, "though I can't really do much to relieve the burden."

"No," Dr. Sykora agreed. "That is my department. And even I don't know if it can be achieved. Well," she gave Shulamis another smile, "we can but try... I'll be here again tomorrow. Goodbye till then." She waved and walked to her car, parked a few yards away.

Shulamis watched her drive away and then walked through the gate, toward the building. As she approached the nursing home, she became suddenly aware of the parcel tucked under her arm. It occurred to Shulamis that she could have asked the doctor whether it was the right thing to encourage Nechy's talent. Oh well, it was too late now. She had gone. And in any case, it would have involved too many explanations. After all, it was Nechy's mother who was Dr.

Sykora's patient, not Nechy herself. She would have decide for herself what to do.

Pushing her way in through the large front doors, Shulamis found Nechy waiting for her in the foyer.

"Oh, Shulamis!" Nechy cried, suppressed excitement in her voice, "the doctor has just left!"

"Yes, I know," Shulamis interrupted her. "I saw her. She spoke to me."

"Really? What do you think of her?"

"She seems nice."

"Yes, she does, doesn't she?" Nechy sounded enthusiastic. "And she's so easy to talk to! I've got this feeling that if anyone can help Mummy, *she* can!"

Shulamis nodded in agreement, glad to see that Nechy had regained some of her sparkle at last. She fervently hoped her friend's faith in this doctor would be justified. She could not bear the thought of another disappointment which would cause Nechy to again become withdrawn.

"I had a long talk with her," Nechy said. "I can't wait to tell you all about it! Come into the dining room and have lunch. Everybody's had theirs already but I waited for you. The cook said she would keep it warm for us." She eyed the brown paper parcel with curiosity but refrained from asking questions.

"Okay," Shulamis said, "but just let me take my things upstairs. I won't be long."

She hurried up to the bedroom and pushed the package to the back of the wardrobe, hiding it behind an empty travel bag. Then she went down and joined Nechy in the dining room.

As they ate their lunch Nechy talked excitedly, telling Shulamis all that had transpired that morning.

"She spent quite a long time alone with Mummy in her room and she told me later that all they talked about was

Mummy's childhood and her life before the war. It made such a difference that she could speak to her in Czech."

"Can't the doctor speak Yiddish?" Shulamis asked.

"No, she isn't Jewish. And even if she was, she wouldn't necessarily be able to speak Yiddish. Most people in Czechoslovakia spoke Czech and German, but Mummy speaks Yiddish because she learned it from her mother, who came originally from Rumania. Anyway, this doctor and her husband, who's also a doctor, were so shocked at the way the Nazis were treating the Jews that they left Czechoslovakia when the Germans invaded and they emigrated to England."

"I see," Shulamis was thoughtful. "You'd think they would stay there to help the Jews."

"How could they? The Nazis had invaded their country and could have forced them to work for them! Rather than do that they ran away. But now they treat anyone who has suffered in the war free of charge. Anyway," Nechy went on, determined to get back to the subject of her mother, "I had a long chat with her afterwards and she told me Mummy began to open up to her after a while and she got quite a picture of the type of person she used to be. She's coming again tomorrow and she'll try to get her to talk about the war…and all that."

"Do you think she'll be able to?"

"I hope so! She'll never succeed in helping her if she doesn't!" There was a desperate note in Nechy's voice.

By now the two girls had finished their meal. They reached for the bentchers lying on the table, bentched and brought their plates back to the kitchen.

"What are we doing this afternoon?" Shulamis asked. "Are we taking your mother out?"

"No, not today," Nechy told her. "She's a bit tired after her session with the doctor. Mrs. Laufer thinks she should have a good rest. We'll go to her room a bit later and chat to her. Or try to…" she added, on a wistful note.

"Well, come upstairs then," Shulamis said. "I want to give you something."

Puzzled and curious, Nechy followed her friend up to their room and watched as she pulled the parcel out of its hiding place.

"Here!" Shulamis said, thrusting it into Nechy's hands. "I got this for you."

Nechy began to tear the paper open, a mystified expression on her face. But the look changed to one of anger as soon as she saw the sketch-pad, pencils and oil-paint sticks the package contained.

Seeing her friend's expression, Shulamis's heart sank. So, her plan had misfired! And now Nechy would draw away from her and shut her out again! Oh, if only she hadn't given way to an impulse and done this stupid thing!

"Shulamis!" Nechy almost hissed at her. "What's the idea? Why have you bought these for me?"

"I-I thought it would give you a push to start sketching again…" Shulamis replied quietly, the color rising in her face. "B-but it's only made you angry. I'm so sorry!" she sounded near to tears.

The anger left Nechy as suddenly as it had come. "Oh, Shulamis, *I'm* sorry!" she cried, contrition in her voice. "I shouldn't have shouted at you like that!" She sat down on her bed, placing Shulamis's purchases beside her. "I know you mean well," she went on, "but you don't understand. It's not that I don't want to draw and paint any more. It's just that I can't! I've tried and I've lost my talent!"

"You can't have!" Shulamis protested. "People are *born* with talents. They can't possibly lose them!"

Nechy sighed dejectedly. "Yes, that's what Yocheved said.

"But she realized she was wrong soon enough!"

"What do you mean?" Shulamis asked, puzzled.

Nechy passed the back of her hand across her forehead, biting her lip as she relived the unpleasant memory. After a few moments she replied. "She made me feel guilty when I told her that I couldn't do the illustrations for the magazine, so I forced myself to try and do it. Well, I knew she wouldn't want them once she saw them and I was absolutely right! I could see she was extremely embarrassed, but she had to tell me that they couldn't use my drawings."

"Oh Nechy!" Shulamis cried with compassion, almost feeling the hurt that Nechy must have felt. "But I don't understand…"

"No, neither do I," Nechy spoke flatly. "All I know is that whatever I try to draw now comes out quite differently to what I have in mind. Sometimes the result is amazingly awful!" Nechy shuddered and shook her head, as if trying to shake the painful reality out of her mind.

"But Nechy," Shulamis spoke softly, feeling she must do something to help Nechy rid herself of this "thing" that had taken hold of her, "perhaps it will be different now that you've got more reason to be hopeful. You were very frustrated before. It's different now!"

Nechy gave another weary sigh. "No," she said, "it's no use. I'd rather *not* try. That way I won't get upset."

She stood up and picked up the contents of the package, shoveling them haphazardly back into the paper wrapping. Going across to the wardrobe, she threw them back inside.

"I'm so sorry, Shulamis. Please don't think I don't appreciate what you're trying to do. I just wish you hadn't wasted your money."

Shulamis waved her hand in a dismissive gesture and quickly busied herself emptying her holdall and tidying the contents. She wanted to tell Nechy that she had more than enough with the pocket-money they received from the Agudah organization that cared for their needs and that she was glad to have something to spend it on.

But, actually, she didn't trust herself to speak. She feared bursting into tears, which would surely only make Nechy feel guilty and guilt was the last thing she could do with now. But, in fact, Shulamis felt terribly disappointed.

"Come on," Nechy said, making a valiant attempt to lighten the atmosphere. "Let's go now for a bit of a walk while Mummy's still resting. Then we'll go and keep her company."

Nechy walked to the cupboard, took out her green wool coat and slipped it on, picking up her scarf, gloves and woolly hat. Shulamis reached for her own outdoor clothes, still lying on the rose-patterned chair she had thrown them onto, and followed her friend out of the room, trying hard to push away her feeling of disappointment and despondency. She had wanted so much to help her friend! Although she knew she was doing so in some way, it all was proving a little too difficult for her. It was all very well for a qualified psychiatrist like Dr. Sykora. She was well trained in dealing with the complexities of people's minds...but for an ordinary person like her...and a young one at that...it was far too complicated!

AN
ENTERTAINING
IDEA

T HE NURSING HOME LOUNGE, TASTEFULLY decorated in shades of peach and lavender, was normally empty in the morning, as the patients typically preferred to stay in their rooms until after lunch. The two girls, therefore, had the place to themselves as they curled up in the deep, soft rose-patterned armchairs, playing word games to pass the time, while Dr. Sykora held her second session with Mrs. Horowitz.

They were busy trying to see who could find the most words with the letters of EPPING FOREST when they noticed the doctor entering the lounge and making her way toward them. Shulamis jumped up immediately, ready to make herself scarce so that Nechy could talk to Dr. Sykora in private, but Nechy, standing up too, put a restricting hand on her arm.

"Please, don't go, Shulamis!" she urged. Then she turned to Dr. Sykora, "It doesn't matter if Shulamis stays, does it?" she asked the doctor.

"Not if *you* don't mind," Dr. Sykora replied with a smile. She signaled to them to sit down again and, pulling another armchair forward, she settled down opposite them. She was wearing a grey suit with a white blouse. Although she looked quite professional, she also looked quite friendly.

For a few moments Dr. Sykora sat without speaking, staring into space with a solemn expression and occasionally shaking her head. Then she said, in an awed voice, "It never ceases to shock me…even though I've heard some of the horrifying facts from other patients. How could they—the beasts!" she shuddered and suddenly became aware of the two girls eyeing her with concern. Forcing a smile, she said, "I'm sorry! Well, as you must have gathered, your mother did speak to me, Nechy, and I think it was quite an ordeal for her…reliving those terrible times! She became quite disturbed afterwards—so much so that I had to call a nurse to give her a sedative.

"Oh!" the single syllable escaped from Nechy, loaded with anxiety. "Shouldn't I go to her?"

"No, she's sleeping now. But she will probably need you when she wakes up, so don't go out. The nurse promised me she would call you when your mother woke up."

Nechy nodded, her bearing tense.

"It's likely your mother will have her nightmares again tonight, even though I instructed the nurse to give her another sedative before she settles down for the night," the doctor went on.

"Was it really necessary to bring up all her bad memories?" Nechy interrupted, her voice now shaking.

"Yes, I'm afraid it was," Doctor Sykora's tone was apologetic. "I can't possibly help her unless I can make a proper assessment of her state of mind. I need to know what she's been through so I can help her. But please try not to be too worried, Nechy. I'm sure we'll get there in the end." She sounded encouraging but Nechy could not suppress a deep sigh.

"I have managed to solve one mystery for you, though," the doctor told her. "You were wondering why your mother seemed to become agitated over your speaking English. Well, I discovered the reason why."

The two girls leaned forward attentively, eager to hear what she had to say.

"Apparently there was a particularly nasty Nazi officer at the camp...it seemed it was he who was responsible for the murder of your grandmother..." Dr. Sykora regarded Nechy sympathetically. Nechy had mentioned to Dr. Sykora that she had been close to her grandmother and had wondered what had happened to her, but could never bring herself to ask her mother about it. "Your mother told me his name," the doctor continued, "but I've forgotten it—something beginning with 'W,' I think. Anyway, although he mostly spoke German there were times when he spoke a language unfamiliar to your mother. When she came to England she realized that he had been speaking English. While waiting for her escort at Dover she saw an elderly lady collide with a man, who expressed his annoyance using the exact expression this Nazi officer often used. It gave her a nasty jolt. Had she been able to, I think she would have turned round and got out of England as fast as she could!"

"Oh, I see." There was a bemused look on Nechy's face. "I never realized how much I was upsetting her! But what can I do? English is the only language I can speak properly nowadays."

"Don't you remember any Yiddish at all?" Dr. Sykora asked her. "I thought all Jewish people can speak Yiddish."

"Well, I can a bit and I try to stick to it when I speak to Mummy, but I can't help the English words creeping in!"

Nechy looked pensive for a moment, then a resolute look crossed her freckled face. "You know what?" she announced, "I know what I'm going to do! I'm going to learn it properly!"

"How?" Shulamis wanted to know. "Who's going to teach you?"

"I don't know. Anybody!" Nechy declared, refusing to allow her enthusiasm to be dampened. "I bet Mrs. Hoffman at school could teach me. And the cook here at the nursing home also speaks Yiddish. So does Mrs. Laufer."

"Yes, you're right!" Shulamis agreed, catching on to Nechy's eagerness. "Maybe Mrs. Laufer would let us help the cook in the kitchen, and she could teach us Yiddish at the same time!"

Dr. Sykora stood up, smiling benignly at the girls. "You're on to the right idea," she said encouragingly. "Well, I'm afraid I must be going now. I'll see you tomorrow."

Shulamis and Nechy accompanied Dr. Sykora to the door and watched as she walked down the path, returning the wave she gave them from the nursing home gate. Then they made their way to Mrs. Laufer's office to put forward their idea.

Watching the cook bustling about the kitchen of the nursing home, Shulamis could not help thinking how different she was from Mrs. Hoffman, the cook at school. Until now Shulamis had always imagined all cooks as big and plump, but Mrs. Ziegelman was quite the opposite. Thin and petite, she reminded Shulamis of a little sparrow. In fact, she had a habit of tilting her head to one side in a bird-like manner and her quick, deft movements gave a similar impression.

As the girls sat at the table, peeling potatoes and carrots, Mrs. Ziegelman stood by the *fleishig* sink, cutting up and cleaning portions of chicken, talking while she worked.

"So, you want to learn Yiddish," she said. "Well, the only way you can learn is if I speak only Yiddish to you...don't you think so?"

The girls nodded their agreement and Mrs. Ziegelman began to chatter away in Yiddish, talking about the menu for the next few days' meals and asking them a lot of questions about themselves. Because Nechy and Shulamis could understand Yiddish, they had little difficulty understanding her. It was only when they had to answer her that problems arose. And they found they could only reply in a mixture of Yiddish and English—although Shulamis threw in a bit of German. Mrs. Ziegelman, however, translated their answers for them, insisting they repeat them correctly in Yiddish.

Nechy found, to her surprise, that many words came back to her during these lessons and as they left the kitchen after one of the sessions she discussed it with Shulamis.

"It's funny that my childhood memory of Yiddish should come back to me now, when Mummy speaking to me didn't have that effect," she mused.

"Yes, I wonder why that is?" Shulamis pondered.

"Maybe it's because Mrs. Ziegelman talked about all sorts of everyday things, which I remember...and Mummy hardly ever does," Nechy suggested, looking thoughtful. "Perhaps I'll ask Dr. Sykora what she thinks, when she comes tomorrow."

The next day, Nechy sat alone in the lounge, waiting for Dr. Sykora to come down after her session with her mother. Shulamis was busy writing letters in their room. As soon as the doctor was seated opposite her, she put forward her theory about her Yiddish learning experience to her.

"Perhaps you're right, Nechy," Dr. Sykora commented, after a moments consideration. "Who knows? But keep on with the lessons and I'm sure you'll soon be able to converse fluently with your mother. Which brings me to something I must talk to you about…I hope you are not going to take this badly." There was a serious expression on the doctor's face.

"W-what is it?" Nechy asked, turning pale. "Is something wrong?"

"No, no!" Dr. Sykora reassured her. "Your mother is doing quite well. It's just that…well…you see, during our talk today it became clear that one of the things hindering her progress is…well…I don't quite know how to put this…your attitude toward her."

"My…attitude?" Nechy gulped, looking at the doctor not comprehending her.

"Your mother remembers you as a happy-go-lucky child, always laughing and singing. When she discovered that you were alive, it was that memory of her cheerful little girl that kept her going until she could join you. And that's how you appeared at first, after your joyful reunion. Then, suddenly, you seemed to become withdrawn and unhappy. This has made her so sad. She was looking to you to pull her out of her misery and now she feels as if she is just a burden to you." As she spoke, Dr. Sykora watched the girl's face crumple up and her eyes fill with tears. It made her feel terribly cruel, but she knew it was essential to get the message across if her patient was to be helped.

Nechy opened her mouth to speak but the words would not come. Instead, the tears brimming in her eyes began to spill out and roll down her cheeks. Dr. Sykora placed her hand on the girl's arm.

"Nechy," she said, her voice full of sympathy, "please don't take it too much to heart. And whatever you do, please try not to feel guilty. Nobody can blame you and you mustn't blame yourself. I know how hard the last few months must have been for you and I am only telling you all this because I know you will do anything to help your mother. But, you know the first step in helping her is to understand her. If we work together, I'm sure we'll soon have her right. Okay?"

Dr. Sykora had moved closer to Nechy and was looking gently into Nechy's eyes. Nechy nodded and gave her a wan smile through her tears. Dr. Sykora stood up and, giving her arm another encouraging pat, took her leave.

"I'll see you tomorrow, Nechy," she said. "And please don't worry. It will all work out all right, you'll see!"

Left alone, Nechy put her head down on the table and wept, hoping no one would come into the lounge. She could not rid herself of this overwhelming feeling of guilt. What had she done? Instead of helping her mother, she had only added to her problems! She didn't think her mother had noticed how difficult she was finding all this. How could she have been so selfish? And how could she now make amends? Oh why had she let her mother down. How could she expect her to trust her now?

Consumed by an awful feeling of shame, Nechy decided she would keep all this to herself and would not even mention it to Shulamis.

Thinking her friend had gone out to post her letters, Nechy climbed the stairs to their room, ready to throw herself onto her bed and pour her misery out onto her pillow. To her consternation, she found Shulamis still in the room, writing. One look at Nechy's face told Shulamis that something was wrong.

"Nechy!" she cried, "whatever is the matter?"

"Uh nothing, really nothing," Nechy replied, making a gigantic effort to appear casual and calm.

"It can't be nothing," Shulamis protested. Nechy's face was so crestfallen and sad.

"I can see you're upset about something! Please do tell me

what's wrong?"

Although Nechy could hear the concern in Shulamis's voice, she was irritated by her friend's intrusion into her privacy, and angry that she was still in the room. So she could not help snapping at her. "There isn't anything wrong! And even if there is, it's none of *your* business!"

Her defenses down, she gave up the pretense and flung herself onto the bed, weeping bitterly.

Shulamis's first inclination was to withdraw and keep out of things, but after a few moments she realized she just could not stand by and watch her friend's unhappiness. Gently, she coerced and cajoled and gradually Nechy's resistance broke down and she poured out her woes to Shulamis.

"It's terrible!" she cried, amid tears. "I'm the one who has been making Mummy so unhappy! Oh, I'll never forgive myself!"

"Nechy! Please stop blaming yourself!" Shulamis cried. "I don't know why you're making such a tragedy out of it. You should be happy!"

"Happy?" Nechy stopped sobbing and gaped aghast. "How can you say that?"

"Don't you see? For one thing, it means that your mother is not completely wrapped up in her own misery. She cares about you and wants you to be happy. And it also means that you hold the key to her recovery! Now you know exactly what you can do to help her!"

"Y-yes, I suppose so." Nechy considered Shulamis's words. "But I still feel so guilty…"

"Well don't!" Shulamis spoke emphatically. "Your guilt helps no one. No one can blame you for reacting as you did. You certainly should stop blaming yourself. But now you have got to start being positive. You must do all you can to cheer your mother up!"

"But how? It isn't easy…"

"I know, but there must be a way!" Shulamis lapsed into a thoughtful silence, her pretty face drawn in concentration. She had become so wrapped up in Nechy's problems lately. She hadn't realized that although her main motives were kindness and concern, all this was fulfilling a need in her too. Essentially a warm, generous person, she had so much to give and had to have someone to give it to. Caring about Nechy gave her a tremendous sense of purpose.

"I know!" she exclaimed, coming out of her reverie, "after lunch, when your mother's awake, we'll go up and sing to her. I bet she'll like that!"

Nechy looked skeptical at first but gradually the idea began to grow on her and, so instead of beating herself up, she began to think productively. By the time they had eaten lunch and were ready to go up to her mother's room, Nechy was full of enthusiasm and determined to act positively on this new information.

Mrs. Horowitz seemed bewildered at first, when the two girls began singing to her, not quite sure what was going on. But after a while a smile began to hover about her lips and when the girls paused for a few moments she asked for more.

"That was lovely!" she said softly in Yiddish, many songs later, giving her daughter's hand a squeeze. "You sing so nicely—both of you!"

"Thanks, Mummy!" Nechy said, returning the squeeze, answering in her awkward Yiddish. "We'll sing to you again tomorrow. Now, what do you think of my Yiddish?"

Mrs. Horowitz inclined her head in a gesture that meant "So, so," but there was an obvious twinkle in her eyes.

The next half-hour Nechy spent trying out her Yiddish, making many mistakes which her mother corrected. There was much giggling from the girls when they made a mistake, interspersed with occasional laughter from Mrs. Horowitz. Shulamis marveled at the difference it made to Mrs. Horowitz's appearance.

Presently, Mrs. Horowitz's eyelids began to droop and Nechy kissed her mother gently on the cheek and crept out with Shulamis.

Once outside the door, Nechy could not wait to express her elation.

"Shulamis, you're a genius! It really worked! Did you see how different she looked? There were times when she seemed really happy!" She almost skipped along the corridor, her step jaunty, and Shulamis felt a warm glow of satisfaction.

On the stairs they met Mrs. Laufer.

"Oh here you are, girls," the matron said, a broad smile on her plump face, "I walked past your mother's room before, Nechy, and I heard beautiful singing. Was that you two?"

"I don't know about beautiful," Nechy replied, blushing, "but we were singing to Mummy. It was Shulamis's idea and Mummy absolutely enjoyed it!"

"I'm sure she did!" Mrs. Laufer exclaimed. "It was a clever thing to do. It will do your mother a lot of good. I must say, I enjoyed it too!" Mrs. Laufer was about to continue her way up the stairs when she stopped suddenly and turned round. "I've just had an idea! How about giving all the patients a bit of entertainment? Maybe you could sing to them tonight, after supper."

The two girls blushed and protested at first, insisting that they would be too embarrassed, but after some persuasion, when they understood how happy it would make the nursing home residents, they agreed.

The little "concert" proved to be a great success. The audience, consisting mainly of elderly women, though there were some younger women, Mrs. Horowitz among them, enjoyed the beautiful, Hebrew songs and applauded enthusiastically, begging for more.

"What a pity you're going back to school the day after tomorrow," Mrs. Laufer commented. "If only we'd hit upon this idea earlier!"

"Yes," Shulamis agreed, a pensive expression on her face. "You know, I've just thought of something…though I'm not sure if Mrs. Langfeld will agree to it…"

"What is it?" Mrs. Laufer and Nechy asked together, both regarding her with curiosity.

"I was just thinking that maybe our school choir could come down here sometimes, on a Sunday afternoon, to sing to the women…"

"Shulamis, that's an absolutely brilliant idea!" Nechy exclaimed eagerly.

"That would be really wonderful!" Mrs. Laufer beamed at them. "Do you think your headmistress will consent to it?"

"Well, we can ask her," Shulamis said, "and if she agrees we can phone you to make arrangements."

"Excellent," the matron nodded. "I do hope it materializes. By the way, Nechy, I must tell you that your mother seems a different person tonight. Dr. Sykora will be pleased when she sees her tomorrow. At least you'll go back to school with an easier mind, knowing that she is surely on the road to recovery."

"Yes, *Boruch Hashem!*" Nechy gave a big sigh. "It's such a relief!"

"Our last full day here," Nechy said, when they awoke the

next morning, as she leaned over to wash her hands.

"Yes. What are we going to do with it?" Shulamis asked.

"Well, I want to spend as much time as I can with Mummy. We can't take her out in the morning because Dr. Sykora is coming, but maybe, if the weather's nice, we'll take her to Epping Forest in the afternoon."

"Great! I can't believe our two weeks are up already. They've gone by so fast. I'd like to go to the forest again before we go back to school." Shulamis washed *negel vasser* and, slipping out of bed, went across to the window and peered out. "The sky is blue. It looks as if it'll be a nice day. I think I'll go into the village this morning, to do a bit of shopping." She didn't say so, but she thought Nechy should have some time alone with her mother before they left.

The weather did indeed turn out to be bright and sunny and Shulamis, having completed her shopping, decided to walk back to the nursing home instead of taking the bus. She thought she might as well enjoy the rustic scenery while she still had the chance. Elmsleigh, of course, was also a picturesque village, filled with old homes and tree-lined streets, but it was different. And besides, they spent most of the time within the school grounds and did not get much opportunity to enjoy the countryside.

Shulamis walked briskly and arrived at the nursing home feeling refreshed by the bracing air. And then she saw a sight that made her heart leap with joy!

Nechy was sitting on one of the garden benches, the brown paper parcel Shulamis had bought lying open beside her, with all the drawing utensil spread out on it. And Nechy, oblivious to everything around her, had the sketch pad on her lap and was sketching for all she was worth, an expression of rapture on her face!

A STRANGE-
LOOKING OBJECT

MRS. LANGFELD REGARDED THE TWO GIRLS IN front of her with interest as she turned their request over in her mind. It was good to see Nechy practically back to her normal self and she was reluctant to do anything that would dampen the girl's enthusiasm at this point. What had happened in Chingford, she wondered, to bring about this change? As far as she could gather, Nechy's mother, although improving, had not made any dramatic strides forward as yet. However, it was obviously a good thing that Shulamis had been there with Nechy and the headmistress was gratified to see that the barrier between the two friends no longer existed.

Now they had come to her with this charming idea and she was impressed and moved by their thoughtfulness. She would have loved to agree outright to their suggestion but something held her back. She knew she tended to be overprotective where her pupils were concerned, but the thought of sending a crowd of them down to Chingford by themselves made her wary. However well-behaved they might be, they were bound to make a bit of noise and would attract a certain amount of attention. Who could tell what dangers might be lurking about…so soon after the war.

She voiced her misgivings to Nechy and Shulamis.

"Couldn't one of the teachers come with us?" Shulamis suggested.

"Yes, I've thought of that. But how can I ask them to give up some of their free time? They have so little of it, as it is."

Noting the disappointment on the girls' faces, Mrs. Langfeld smiled encouragingly at them. "But I will ask them at the next staff meeting," she promised. "You never know, someone might volunteer. It's such a lovely idea…it would be a shame to give it up."

When, indeed, she outlined the plan to her staff a few days later, she was overwhelmed by their enthusiastic response to it.

A warm feeling of satisfaction came over her as she regarded them all seated around the table. How wonderfully suppportive they were! Mrs. Gold, who taught English and History, was indeed a treasure. Living in Chesham, she was the only teacher who did not live in but made the journey every day without fail. And Miss Katz and Miss Ellberger, two of the *limudei kodesh* teachers, were quite young and their dedication to their jobs was touching. Miss Hertzman, too, was a reliable member of the staff. She taught math and often put in extra hours to give some of the slower girls additional attention. Then there was Miss Feinbaum who had only joined them that term but had quickly fit in. It was good to see them all so eager!

"What a sweet thought!" Miss Katz exclaimed. "I'd be glad to take the girls down there!" It was typical of Devora Katz to be the first to volunteer, being, perhaps, the most dedicated of

Migdal Binoh's teachers.

"So would I!" Miss Hertzman echoed, putting up her hand as if she were one of the pupils.

"And I!"…"Me too!"…"Count me in!"…the voices of the entire staff merged together, each one expressing eagerness to take part in the venture.

Mrs. Langfeld laughed as she held up her hand to restore order. "Thanks, all of you!" she said. "Your enthusiasm is so gratifying. However, now I'm left with another problem. You're all so willing to go, I just won't know whom to choose!"

"Well, if it becomes a regular thing we'll all get a turn," Miss Hertzman pointed out.

"True," the headmistress agreed, smiling. "I'll tell Shulamis or Nechy to contact Mrs. Laufer, the matron of the nursing home, and we'll make the necessary arrangements."

"I must say," Mrs. Gold commented, "I was amazed at the difference in Nechy! She's seems to have regained her old cheerful disposition, hasn't she?"

"Yes," Miss Ellberger agreed. "It was just awful to see what happened to her once her mother was discovered. She had grown so miserable and withdrawn. It just wasn't like her!" Being the youngest of the teachers, Miss Ellberger was often in the habit of identifying herself with the girls emotionally.

"I never knew her before," Miss Feinbaum, the new art teacher remarked, "all I know is that I'd been told how artistic she is and when I saw her work I had quite a shock. Her drawings were…well…quite odd, to say the least. And then she stopped coming into lessons altogether." She tapped on her slightly protruding teeth with her pencil, a mannerism she often adopted when perplexed.

"Well, I hope she'll start taking an interest in her art again," Mrs. Langfeld said. "I must say, I missed her illustrations in the last issue of the magazine!"

"I'd like to see some of her work," Miss Feinbaum said. "Is there anything around for me to see?"

"I think there's a copy of one of the earlier magazines here." Mrs. Gold stood up and walked over to a cupboard in the alcove, opening a drawer and rummaging about. "Ah, here it is!"

She handed the magazine to Miss Feinbaum, who scanned it with interest.

"These are really good!" she commented, her eyes widening. "I think this girl really shows talent. I must encourage her to develop it."

"Well, take care not to pressure her," Mrs. Langfeld warned. "Her relationship with her mother is still delicate and I wouldn't want anything to set her back again!"

Shulamis's thoughts also harbored hopes of Nechy regaining her old self. She hovered protectively around her friend, making sure no one upset her with too much probing. She knew that all Nechy wanted was to get back to normal and put the difficult phase she had been through behind her, but this would be impossible if people began to make comments. Fortunately the girls, though often eyeing Nechy with curiosity, steered clear of asking too many questions about her time at the nursing home while Nechy was about, though many of them bombarded Shulamis with questions when her friend was out of earshot.

"Even though I may have been upset at the time, I'm glad you went with Nechy," Simi Korwich remarked. "It seems to have changed her dramatically! Whatever did you do to make all that difference?"

"Nothing much," Shulamis answered, her tone non-committal. "Anyway, I'm sure you and Etty had loads of fun together!"

"We did, as a matter of fact," Simi replied, disappointed at her failure to draw Shulamis out.

There was one person, however, to whom Shulamis was more forthcoming. She knew that Yocheved was not questioning her out of curiosity, but interest and concern. Yocheved, after all, had always been like a big sister to them, being the oldest of the four orphans. She found herself telling the older girl all that had transpired at Chingford. There was relief and admiration in Yocheved's voice as she put a hand on Shulamis's shoulder.

"You've done an amazingly good job," she said, "and *Boruch Hashem*, you've had a lot of *siyata dishmaya*! Now it's up to all of us to encourage Nechy as much as we can!"

Etty, too, was bursting with curiosity, but knew better than to mention the subject to either of the two girls. Convinced that Mrs. Langfeld must know something of what went on, she tried to extract the information from her as she went to bid her mother good night.

"I really couldn't tell you," Mrs. Langfeld said. "All I know is that it's such a relief to see Nechy back to her usual self, and that's good enough for me!"

After Etty went out, Mrs. Langfeld sat in her office pondering the situation. She felt it wasn't really important to know why things had turned out as they did. The thing that mattered now was to keep the girls on an even keel. Now, perhaps, everything would get back to normal and the smooth running of the school could be resumed.

However, that night Mrs. Langfeld did not have a restful sleep. She dreamed that the very next day a dramatic event would occur that would upset her quiet little school all over again!

In the Junior common room Pearlie Abel stuck a stamp onto the envelope she had just addressed and stood up.

"Would you come with me to mail my letter?" she asked her friend, Feigy Beck.

"It's freezing out," Feigy replied, looking up from the book she was reading. "I'm really not in the mood now to *schlepp* to the cloakroom to get my coat, just to post a letter! Has it got to be today?"

"Yes, it's a birthday card for my little sister and I want her to get it on her birthday."

"I don't mind coming with you," Mindy Spiegel volunteered. She was always willing to help other girls. "I'm getting a bit stiff sitting here. Perhaps we can go for a bit of a stroll at the same time."

"Good idea! I'll come too!" Tzippy Weissland stood up as she spoke. Her red hair was, as usual, a mess. But she had the brightest smile.

With Pearlie leading the way, the three third-formers fetched their wool coats and warm hats and, wrapping up warmly, made their way out of the school grounds, toward the post box a few yards down the lane.

Tzippy, who always needed something to do—even while walking—took a ball out of her pocket and began to bounce it as they walked. They reached the post box and Pearlie examined the sign underneath the opening.

"Next collection 5 p.m," she read out. "Good!" she said, thrusting her envelope inside, "I haven't missed the last p—"

Her words were interrupted by a cry from Tzippy.

"—Oh no! I've lost the ball! It's gone into the bushes somewhere!" She began to thrash about in the bushes, pulling frantically at the branches. "I must find it. It isn't my ball. It belongs to Zeesie Schonberg and I promised her I'd bring it back!"

The other two began to help in the search but, after ten minutes of fruitless rummaging, Pearlie said, "It's no use. You'll never find it. Let's go back. You can buy Zeesie another ball."

It was at that moment that Mindy, searching a little further away, called out. "Hey! Come over here a minute! There's something extremely strange here!"

Running over to join her, Pearlie and Tzippy stared in surprise at the spot Mindy was indicating.

"W-what do you think it is?" Mindy asked, a tremor in her voice.

The thing, which was half buried in the ground, was obviously no ordinary object. The girls eyed it for a few moments with awed expressions. Then Mindy repeated her question.

"I don't know," Pearlie said. "It might be a bomb!"

"Don't be silly!" Tzippy declared haughtily, "Of course it's not a bomb!"

"How do you know?" Pearlie demanded defensively.

"Well, it stands to reason!" Tzippy remarked, "if it was a bomb it would have exploded, wouldn't it? It's been here for ages! Look, it's all rusty." She touched the tail of 'The Object' gingerly, displaying a thin layer of rust on the fingertip of her glove.

"I bet it's a piece of a plane," Mindy announced. "There must have been an airplane crash near here once…or maybe it's a bit of a German plane that was shot down," her voice took on a melodramatic tone as she enlarged upon her theory, enjoying the rapt attention of her audience. "I think we ought to take it to the police. It might be a vital piece of evidence or something!"

"How can we?" Tzippy wanted to know. "It's stuck firmly in the ground."

"Between the three of us we should be able to dislodge it," Mindy insisted. "Come on, let's try!"

It turned out to be a less difficult task than they had imagined. Though firmly embedded, only a third of the object was buried and a few determined tugs from the three girls soon unearthed it completely. They studied it as it lay on the ground in front of them. Its cylinder-shaped body was about two feet long and not more than three or four inches wide. As far as they could see through the rust it was made of steel and painted dark gray. At the nose end a small oblong piece protruded and at the other end there was a steel tail about nine inches long and five inches wide.

"It looks a bit like a mackerel, doesn't it?" Pearlie commented. "I think you're right about it being part of a plane. What shall we do with it?"

"Take it to the police, of course!" Mindy said in a matter-of-fact tone.

They bent down to pick it up. "It's quite heavy," Tzippy said. "I don't see how we can carry it all the way to the police station. We don't even know exactly where the police station is. Let's take it to Mrs. Langfeld. It's better if she phones the police to pick it up.

The others agreed with her and together they carried their find a few yards up the lane and into the school grounds.

As they approached the school building they saw Mrs. Langfeld herself emerging through the front door. They hurried toward her, the strange object resting heavily on their arms.

"Mrs. Langfeld, look what we've found!" Pearlie called. "We think it's part of a plane that must have crashed..."

"And we wanted to take it to the police," Mindy took up.

"—but we decided to bring it to you instead," Tzippy finished off for them.

By now they were standing right in front of the headmistress, who stared at the object, a look of absolute horror on her face.

Turning deathly pale, she snatched the thing from their hands. "Get straight into the building!" she hissed at the girls, "and don't tell a soul about this! Go on! Run!!"

And to the shock and bewilderment of the three girls, she began to run toward the gate with the object in her hands.

It had not taken Mrs. Langfeld long to realize that the object that the girls had unearthed was nothing less than a German bomb!

She had heard that some of the bombs the Germans had dropped over England had landed in hidden places and failed to explode. This was obviously one of those bombs and now that it had been disturbed it might go off at any moment!

Aware that she must get it away from the school as soon as possible, she ran as fast as she could, even though the bomb was heavy and her legs felt like jelly. She knew she was carrying her life in her hands and she tried to think of some *Tehillim* to say, but nothing would come to mind. All the same she said a silent prayer in her heart that the bomb would not explode. True, the girls had pulled it out of the ground and carried along without mishap, but there was no knowing when it could go off.

She knew she was doing the right thing, even though she was risking her life. If, *chas veshalom*, it should blow up in her hands, she would be killed instantly and would probably hardly feel a thing. If, however, the building would be blown up, the girls…her precious charges…she shuddered, pushing the unbearable thought out of her head.

Suddenly, without warning, thoughts of her late husband, Aryeh, sprang up in her mind. Aryeh had been doing fire-watching duty in London during the war when a bomb had hit the area. He hadn't been blown up by the explosion, but had been killed by falling debris from the demolished buildings around. Too wrapped up in her own sense of bereavement, she hadn't really thought of what he had suffered, but now a gruesome picture rose up in front of her, adding to the panic and terror she already felt.

She reached the gate and sped down the lane, realizing, suddenly, that she had no idea where the girls had found the bomb. There hadn't really been time to ask them. The bushes near the post box looked as if they had been tampered with, but there were no spaces in them that looked big enough. Then, a little further down, she spotted it. This, she was sure, was the spot! Peering down into it, she saw a dent in the ground that was the exact shape of the nose of the bomb! Sighing with relief, she bent down and, with great gentleness, replaced the bomb, praying fervently that the contact with the ground would not detonate the fuse!

Her mission completed, she straightened up and rubbed her aching arms. Only now did she realize how heavy the object had been! Suddenly, a feeling of calm enveloped her and she knew instinctively that there was no immediate threat. The thing was not about to blow up.

"Thank you, *Hashem*, thank you!" she said aloud, as she turned and hurried back to the school to telephone the police.

DANGER AVERTED

PEARLIE, TZIPPY AND MINDY WERE STILL standing in the hall, puzzlement and concern written on their faces, when Mrs. Langfeld rushed in. Not bothering to stop and explain, the head-mistress beckoned to them to follow her as she hurried into her office and picked up the telephone.

The three girls gaped, their eyes wide open, as they heard her words.

"Is that the police?" she said, urgency in her tone. Then, after a pause in which someone of authority had obviously answered her request, "This is Mrs. Langfeld of Migdal Binoh School, Woodcroft Lane. We've found an unexploded bomb not far away from here...three of my pupils discovered it...yes, I have seen it!...yes, I'm quite sure!....evacuate the pupils and staff? Officer, where could I take over a hundred girls?...The cellar is probably the safest place. We were told to use it during the war in the event of an air-raid...Yes, I'll do that immediately...and I'll come out and show your men the spot...no, I insist! They'll have difficulty finding it otherwise...well, it hasn't exploded so far, so it's hardly likely to, unless it's touched."

Thanking the officer, she replaced the receiver hastily and began to walk toward the door. "Come quickly," she told the three girls, "we must get everyone into the cellar as soon as possible. But there is just one thing. You are not to tell *anyone* that you actually picked up the bomb and carried it here! Do you promise me that?"

"Yes, Mrs. Langfeld," the girls nodded solemnly, the awed expressions still on their faces.

There was a certain amount of panic and confusion as the entire school gathered in the hall, in answer to the fire bell. At first everyone thought it was just a routine fire drill since there was no evidence of a fire—no smoke or smell of burning—but the urgency in Mrs. Langfeld's manner soon made it obvious that some kind of emergency was at hand.

The headmistress blew her whistle to gain attention and the girls' talking subsided immediately. When she spoke her voice was calm.

"We are all going down into the cellar," she said. "There is *no* time to explain now, but once we are all down there I will tell you what all this is about. There is no cause for alarm or panic and I want you all to go down in an orderly manner. No pushing and shoving, please!" She nodded to Mrs. Gold, who led the way. The girls, obeying the order they were given, filed quietly down the stairs and, within five minutes, pupils and teachers were assembled in the safety of the cellar.

It was a vast place with whitewashed walls and brick supporting pillars. It was clean and well-kept, in spite of a slightly musty smell. All the sides near the walls were used for storage but the central area was still furnished with the trestle tables and benches that had been placed there when a Jewish school from London had been evacuated in the building during the war. Mrs. Langfeld had been one of the teachers of that school, and when she had acquired the house, then called Kettering Manor, after the war to open her school, she had decided to leave the tables and benches where they were, in case of an emergency. Now she was glad she had made that decision.

When the girls were all seated Mrs. Langfeld blew her whistle again, to quiet the hubbub of voices caused by over a hundred girls speculating or expressing puzzlement to one another.

"I told you all I would give you an explanation," she said, her voice echoing strangely, "but I must hurry back upstairs for a while, so Mrs. Gold will explain everything." She nodded to Mrs. Gold, who was eyeing her with concern. "Don't worry, I'm sure I'll be safe," she assured her in a low voice, before turning and hurrying up the stairs. She was aware of her daughter, Etty calling anxiously after her and would have liked to reassure her too, but there was no time to be lost. The police and the bomb-disposal unit must, no doubt, have arrived by now and would be wondering where to start looking for the bomb.

Sure enough, as she made her way toward the school gates, she could see a policeman searching about in the bushes on the other side of the road, just outside the school grounds. She began to hurry toward him when she became aware of running footsteps behind her.

"Mrs. Langfeld! Come back! Too dangerous it is!" A voice with a German accent called out and Mrs. Langfeld, turning briefly, saw the matron, Miss Zemmel, running after her.

"Miss Zemmel, please go back!" she called desperately, not daring to stop.

But Miss Zemmel, disregarding her order, caught up with her as she reached the gate.

Ignoring her for the moment, Mrs. Langfeld called out to the policeman, "It's not in there, Officer. It's further down! I'll show you!"

She ran on, toward the post-box, with the policeman and Miss Zemmel hard on her heels, and pointed out the spot. Another policeman joined them and the two men peered down into the bushes together, both straightening up abruptly, as if they had been stung. Then the second policeman signaled toward a green army truck, parked nearby and two men, wearing helmets and protective clothing emerged. They too peered into the bushes and nodded.

"It's an SC 10! No doubt it's an unexploded bomb left from the war. We've found a few of these in villages nearby." one of the men announced. "We'll have to try and defuse it. But you'll have to clear the area first," he told the two police officers.

While all this was going on Mrs. Langfeld was engaged in a slight struggle with Miss Zemmel, who was frantically trying to pull her away from the danger zone.

"Please, Mrs. Langfeld!" she begged. "It is not safe! Come with me quickly back!"

"Yes, Miss Zemmel...I will in a minute. Just let me make sure they find it first."

"But meanwhile an explosion perhaps there will be!" the matron cried, agitated. "We will both be killed!"

"No, Miss Zemmel, I don't think there is any danger until they start defusing it."

"Ja, Ja! You say that...but how can you know?"

"Because..." Mrs. Langfeld began and stopped short.

Should she tell Miss Zemmel the true facts, she wondered, and decided that she would. Although German was the native language of both women—Miss Zemmel had come from Berlin and Mrs. Langfeld from Vienna—they had agreed to converse in English only while at the school. Now, however, Mrs. Langfeld decided it would be advisable to speak German. "Because," she repeated in German, "I myself have had it in my hands. Three of the girls found it and brought it to me and I quickly ran out with it and put it back where they found it."

Miss Zemmel gasped. "But Mrs. Langfeld! You took a big risk! You could have…"

"Yes, I know," the headmistress interrupted, "but I had no choice. And *Boruch Hashem,* nothing happened. But please, don't tell anyone what I have told you. It must be kept secret!"

"Yes, of course. But why?"

"First of all," Mrs. Langfeld explained, "I wouldn't like any of the parents to hear about it. They'll get a terrible shock just thinking what *could* have happened! And besides, with all the publicity this will attract, I don't want reporters to come along to question the girls. I don't think it will be good for them."

"Yes, maybe you are right," the matron nodded sagely. "Don't worry, I will keep it to myself!"

By now a small crowd had gathered and one of the policemen began to bellow at them to get away as fast as possible.

"You had better evacuate the inhabitants of all the houses in this lane," one of the bomb-disposal experts instructed the police officers. "These SC 10s are pretty powerful!"

"Help!" The cry came from Mr. Campbell, who was amongst the crowd. "I live in the cottage next door and my wife is still in there!"

"Well get her out!" the policeman cried. "I'll radio for a patrol car to come immediately and take you to safety."

Mr. Campbell began to run clumsily down toward his cottage, his usually neat hair standing up in an unruly manner. The other policeman turned to Mrs. Langfeld.

"You must be the headmistress, who telephoned us. What about your pupils and staff? Are they safe?"

"Hopefully," Mrs. Langfeld told him. "It would have taken far too long to evacuate them so we have taken them down to the cellar, which was used as a shelter during the war. They should be safe there."

The policeman, looking skeptical, shrugged his shoulders and said, "Well, I would get down there myself, if I were you. We'll give you quarter-of-an-hour before we start. Will that be enough?"

Mrs. Langfeld nodded. "Please let us know when the danger is over," she said and, taking Miss Zemmel by the arm, began to run back into the school grounds.

Once inside the building she told Miss Zemmel to go down ahead of her and she ran into the Assembly Hall, where she grabbed a pile of *sifrei Tehillim* before making her own way down into the cellar.

The air of tension and anxiety in the dimly-lit cellar eased considerably as pupils and teachers began to recite *Tehillim* together. There were not enough *Tehillim* to go round but, with two or three girls sharing one between them, they managed to repeat the words after Mrs. Langfeld. She was glad she had chosen to read them out aloud as it prevented her from listening out for the explosion she half expected to hear at any moment. But the words of *Dovid Hamelech* had a calming effect on her too and she soon felt more relaxed.

Loud rapping sounds, followed by the ringing of the doorbell, made her jump and there were startled gasps from most of the gathering. A quick glance at her watch told Mrs. Langfeld that half-an-hour had elapsed since she had joined the rest of the school in the cellar.

"That must be the police," she announced. "It seems the danger must be over. But," she held up her hand as some of the girls rose from their seats, "remain seated, please. You will have to stay down here until I have made sure. You can carry on saying *Tehillim* meanwhile."

She ran up the cellar steps, praying that she was right about the danger being past. She crossed the hall, aware that the knocking and doorbell-ringing had started again. Obviously the policeman was growing impatient. But, as she flung the front-door open, she saw, to her relief, that he was smiling.

He bowed with a flourish. "Sergeant Bigley at your service, Ma'am. Just want to let you know that it's all O.K. now!" he said affably. "Those bomb-disposal blokes are astonishing! They worked away, calmly and efficiently, when all the time they know their lives are in danger! Apparently, that was a powerful bomb! And the fuse was still live. I don't know! I take my hat off to them, I really do!"

Mrs. Langfeld astutely pointed out that he and his colleague had been equally courageous, staying there while the defusing work was in process.

"Your lives were at risk too, you know," she remarked.

"So they were," Sergeant Bigley replied, blushing slightly, "so they were. Nice of you to say so. But there you are, Ma'am. Duty's duty!"

"Well, thank you for letting me know," the headmistress began, preparing to close the door. She was longing to release her pupils and staff from their temporary prison. And she felt such a powerful feeling of relief—she hadn't realized how scared she had been until now that it was all over. She needed to sit down for a few minutes and get her bearings.

The Sergeant, however, showed no sign of taking his

leave. He stepped into the hall and took out a notebook and pencil.

"Have to make out a report," he explained. "Would you mind filling me in with the details. How the bomb was discovered and so on."

Mrs. Langfeld winced slightly. What was she going to tell him? And how long could she leave everyone in that depressing cellar, wondering what was happening.

"Just a moment," she said, "I'd like to tell my teachers to bring the girls up from the cellar—they've been there long enough, I think!—and then we'll go into my office."

Sergeant Bigley nodded understandingly and waited patiently while the headmistress went to the cellar door and called down instructions. Then she returned and beckoned to him to follow her into the office.

The stampede and the babble of voices, as the girls walked past the slightly open office door, made conversation impossible for a while. But as they waited for the noise to subside, Mrs. Langfeld welcomed the delay. She wasn't quite sure what to tell the policeman. How would she be able to conceal some of the truth without actually telling any lies?

"Three of the girls discovered it and came to tell me about it," she said, feeling her way carefully round her words. "Of course, I realized at once what it was and telephoned you immediately," she ended simply, spreading her hand out in a gesture that seemed to say 'that's all there is to it.'

"Mmm...." Sergeant Bigley muttered, scribbling onto his pad. "And the names of the three girls...?"

"Is it really necessary for me to tell you?" Mrs. Langfeld asked. "I would prefer not to."

"Oh?" The Sergeant eyed her quizzically. "Why is that?"

"Various reasons," the headmistress replied. "News travels fast and if their parents hear about it they might become upset, even though nothing actually happened to them. And besides that, you know what things are like in a girls' school, officer. They'll end up feeling like heroines, especially if newspaper reporters turn up asking to interview them. I don't encourage that kind of thing here."

"I see," The sergeant closed his notepad and replaced the pencil. "I won't press you then. In any case, it doesn't really matter who they are. Well, thank you, Ma'am. I'll get back to the station and make my report before I go off duty. It's been quite an afternoon, hasn't it!" he added with feeling.

When he had gone Mrs. Langfeld breathed a giant sigh of relief. It had been quite easy, after all! She was sure she had done the right thing. After all, it hadn't been necessary to disclose more than she had done and no one need ever know how close to disaster they had come!

Her feeling of complacency was shattered early next morning when she answered a ring at the door.

"Mrs. Langfeld? My name is Jeremy Oakes, from the Elmsleigh Gazette."

Oh no! she thought, not a reporter already! Well, she would send him packing!

But his next words almost sent her reeling.

"I understand you actually handled the bomb, Mrs. Langfeld, and so did three of your pupils. Do you think I could have a few words with them?"

A BAFFLING
MYSTERY

RS. LANGFELD STARED AT HIM FOR A MOMENT, before composing herself quickly. She could see she would have to watch her step. But how, she asked herself, could this reporter possibly have found out?

"I don't know where you got this nonsense from!" she said sharply.

"You mean it isn't true?" the young reporter asked, disappointment on his face.

Mrs. Langfeld evaded the question. "I have already given the police officer the facts," she told him firmly.

"Which are?" Jeremy Oakes persisted, running a hand through his curly, blonde hair.

"Which are," the headmistress repeated, "that three girls discovered the bomb in the bushes, while searching for a ball, and reported their find to me."

"And what did you do?"

"Telephoned the police, of course! What would *you* have done?"

The reporter grinned. "The same, I suppose. But did you phone them immediately or go and see it for yourself first?"

"Mr...er...I've forgotten your name," Mrs. Langfeld's tone was impatient, "I hardly see the point in all these questions and I certainly haven't the time to stand here answering them! If you want to write an interesting story for your paper why don't you write about the skill and courage the bomb-disposal experts displayed, defusing the bomb. That should make good reading, at least!"

"Maybe," Mr. Oakes looked a little put out. "But couldn't I just have a quick word with the three girls...?"

"Most definitely not!" the headmistress declared emphatically. "This kind of publicity is *not* encouraged at our school!"

"I see." With a somewhat dejected air the reporter turned slightly, preparing to go. "My editor will not be pleased. He seemed to be under the impression that the bomb was actually *handled!* Oh, well..." he sighed and shrugged, "someone's got something wrong somewhere, it seems. Good morning, Mrs. Langfeld. Sorry to have troubled you."

Mrs. Langfeld closed the door gently behind him with a sigh of relief. But she could not stop the alarm bells ringing in her head. Who had given the information to the Elmsleigh Gazette? Of course, it could have been a bluff—the sort of trick journalists were prone to—but she didn't think it was likely in this case. The facts were too near the truth!

Her perplexity grew as the morning wore on, after she had been forced to send away three more reporters. Each one had arrived, furnished with information that was uncannily accurate and had also requested an interview with the three girls involved.

Resolving to get to the bottom of this puzzle, Mrs. Langfeld summoned the three girls to her office.

"Somehow," she told them, "the fact that the three of you

and I myself—all handled the bomb, has leaked out and I'm wondering how that happened. Now, I want to know the truth. Did any of you tell *anyone* about it?"

"No, Mrs. Langfeld!" they all responded simultaneously, the spontaneity of their reply convincing her of their honesty. "We didn't even say a word when everyone was wondering why we were going down to the cellar," Pearlie added meaningfully. "Well, is it possible that someone saw you?" the headmistress pursued her interrogation. "Try to remember."

She watched intently as the girls, their brows furrowed in deep concentration, cast their minds back for a few moments. Then Tzippy shook her head.

"No, I'm sure there was no one about," she said decisively. "I remember looking around to see if someone could tell us what it was."

"And I remember now that I thought we must look a bit suspicious, carrying that thing together," Mindy announced, a note of triumph in her voice, "and I looked back to see if anyone was watching.

"Hmm," Mrs. Langfeld was thoughtful. "I suppose Mr. Campbell couldn't have seen you from his gate?" she suggested.

"I don't think so," Pearlie remarked. "I saw him and his wife getting out of a taxi a few minutes earlier, with a huge box of groceries which he carried in through the gate and then he seemed to disappear from our line of vision, so he couldn't very well have seen us either.

"So that rules him out," Mrs. Langfeld said, a little disappointed. Having Mr. Campbell as the culprit would have simplified matters. It would have been just like him to spread tales and the whole thing might have made sense. But as things were, the matter still remained a baffling mystery.

"I expect we'll never know how it got out," she told the

girls, "but I hope I can still rely on you to keep the facts to yourselves."

The girls, gratified by the headmistress's trust in them, gave their assurance readily.

After she had dismissed them Mrs. Langfeld sat at her desk, twirling her pen absently, as she pondered over the situation. The girls, she knew, were telling the truth. And even if they had told someone there was no way it could have reached outside the school in such a short time. Even Miss Zemmel, whom she trusted implicitly, would not have had the chance to impart her knowledge to the outside world. How, then, did it reach the ears of all those newspaper editors?

Her mind began to explore all the possibilities. Could anyone have overheard her telling Miss Zemmel? Even if someone had, she had spoken German and she doubted any of the people near her outside were familiar with the language. The small crowd had consisted mainly of children, and among the adults she had recognized Mr. Campbell and a deaf old lady who lived on the other side of the lane, plus a few rather illiterate local inhabitants. The two policemen and the bomb-disposal men, even if they understood German, were not close enough and in any case were too busy.

And yet, someone had obviously seen or heard something.

Pearlie Abel had seen Mr. and Mrs. Campbell go in through their gate with their groceries and was convinced they could not have seen them carrying the bomb and she, herself, had automatically made sure there was no one in sight when she had returned it. There was still one possible explanation. Perhaps the Campbells had spied them from an upstairs window of their cottage.

Overcome by a desire to check out this possibility, she stood up and, taking a jacket off a hook on the door, slipped it and went outside.

A blustery wind was blowing, making an untidy mess of Mrs. Langfeld's usually immaculate *sheitel*, but she was too intent on her purpose to bother about it. As she reached the spot where the bomb had been she glanced in the direction of 'The Willows' and realized that, due to a curve in the lane, the cottage was not visible from that point. Even if Mr. Campbell had come through his gate, he would not have been able to see anything.

She walked a little further, passing the bend in the lane, and looked up at the cottage. There were no upstairs windows facing her direction at all. So, that rules out the Campbells, she thought wryly, feeling rather foolish.

At that moment Mr. Campbell himself came down the path and spotted her. Eyebrows raised at her slightly unruly appearance, he raised his hat and nodded. Mrs. Langfeld lifted her hand in a halfhearted wave and hurried away. She had no wish to make polite conversation and she certainly did not want to have to make some excuse for standing around, staring up at his house.

"Mummy, you look all wind blown! Wherever have you been?" Etty, who was in the hall when Mrs. Langfeld entered, stared at her mother in surprise.

But Mrs. Langfeld, hastily patting her *sheitel* straight with her hands, did not answer. She hurried to her office, where she could hear the telephone ringing.

She grabbed the receiver hurriedly.

"H-hello," she panted breathlessly, "Migdal Binoh School."

"Mrs. Langfeld? Horace Dobson here."

Mrs. Langfeld's heart sank. A call from Mr. Dobson usually spelled trouble.

"Yes, Mr. Dobson?" she said, apprehensively.

"I've just heard something extraordinary disturbing, Mrs. Langfeld! I'm hoping you will tell me it isn't true."

"I can only do that if I know what it is," Mrs. Langfeld tried to sound calm and cool, though she could sense what he was leading up to.

"It has come to my ears," the pompous voice came through the ear-piece, "that the bomb that was discovered outside your school was actually brought into the premises by some of your pupils, and that you..." the word "you" was loaded with accusation, "took it into your hands and carried it out of the grounds!"

"I don't know who told you that!" Once again the headmistress found herself carefully guarding her words.

"You mean it's not true?" Mr. Dobson sounded deflated. "But..."

Mrs. Langfeld suddenly felt tired of fobbing people off the whole time, especially as it was against her principles to tell lies. She had managed, till now, to avoid actually doing that, but withholding the truth, nevertheless. What did it really matter after all, if the true facts were known?

She sighed wearily. "It's quite true," she said resignedly. "I just can't understand how you came to hear of it. Who told you?"

"That is neither here nor there," he replied haughtily. "Mrs. Langfeld, I'm surprised at you! Do you realize what might have happened?"

"Indeed I *do*!" Mrs. Langfeld said emphatically, encouraged by her conviction that she had done the right thing. "And do *you* realize what would have happened if the bomb had exploded in the school grounds?"

"But you risked your life!" Mr. Dobson cried.

"I had no choice," Mrs. Langfeld said simply.

Mr. Dobson could not help admiring this courageous headmistress, but he had telephoned to reprimand her and reprimand her he would! He would *not* have his authority undermined!

"You should have called the police and evacuated the school!" he said sternly. "And that is not only *my* opinion! I'm afraid it will not look good in the eyes of the Education Committee when they read my monthly report."

Mrs. Langfeld sensed disaster and strove to avert it. "Mr. Dobson," she said persuasively, "is it necessary to publish the full story? I merely told the police that three girls discovered it and reported it to me, whereupon I contacted them."

"Why did you tell them that?" Mr. Dobson asked sharply.

"Because I wanted to avoid any kind of publicity that might turn the girls' heads. I don't think it would be good for them educationally. And besides, I would be happier if the parents of these girls did not hear of it just yet. It might cause some sort of delayed shock for them."

"Hmm," Mr. Dobson was thoughtful for a moment. He suddenly had visions of panicky parents withdrawing their daughters from the school. And where would that leave him? He was the one who had supported the school, against a certain amount of opposition from the local educational authorities. A sudden drop in the number of pupils would cast serious doubts upon the wisdom of his judgement.

He coughed and cleared his throat. "Very well, Mrs. Langfeld," he said, his tone a little subdued, "I will stick to the version you gave the police in my report. But please, be more careful in future!"

Giving her assurance, Mrs. Langfeld replaced the receiver with a feeling of indignation and irritation. Really! One would have thought she herself had planted the bomb there!

But the puzzle still remained. Who was it who knew the full story and had given out the information?

A strange feeling began to gnaw at her brain—a feeling that this had happened before. Hadn't there had been another time when Mr. Dobson had been told something she had preferred him not to know?

Suddenly her head cleared and she remembered. It had been the matter of her lack of qualifications.

The more she thought of it the more she was convinced that Mr. Campbell was the trouble maker. But how was it possible? she wondered. How could he possibly have known?

SILVER LININGS

T HE BOMB INCIDENT SOON BECAME A NINE-DAY-wonder as the school swung back into its normal routine of lessons and social activities. The girls no longer talked about it as they studied for tests or organized Shabbos socials and motzei Shabbos entertainment. Even the few girls who had written home about the bomb had had Mrs. Langfeld calm their parents down. Mrs. Langfeld began to relax a little, though from time to time she would puzzle over the mystery, wishing she knew the answer.

The telephone call she received a few weeks after the event, therefore, came as a bit of a shock to her.

"Mrs. Langfeld?" a breezy female voice came over the line.

"Y-yes?" the headmistress replied warily.

"Buckinghamshire County Council Offices," the voice said crisply. "Hold the line a moment. Miss Hall would like to have a word with you." Mrs. Langfeld's heart began to beat faster as she listened to a series of pips, followed by a click.

A deep woman's voice came across, sounding efficient and

businesslike.

"Miss Hall from the Education Department speaking. Mrs. Langfeld, I'll come straight to the point. We had a telephone call recently, giving us certain facts about the incident of the bomb near your school that do not quite tally with Mr. Dobson's report. Can you throw some light on the matter?"

"Not knowing what you have been told, how can I?" Mrs. Langfeld retorted, hoping the tremor in her voice was not detectable.

There was a slight pause before Miss Hall replied. "This might take too long to discuss over the telephone. Maybe it would be best if I called on you. When would it be convenient?"

A time was arranged for the following day and when the tall, big-boned woman was ushered into her office Mrs. Langfeld regarded her without surprise. Her appearance matched her voice exactly. Her slightly graying, straw-colored hair was swept away from her face and secured behind her ears with two combs. She wore an oatmeal tweed suit with a cream blouse and brown leather lace-up shoes. A large snake-skin shoulder-bag hung from her shoulder and tucked under one arm was a cumbersome file, which she placed on the desk before sitting down on the chair Mrs. Langfeld indicated.

"I have Mr. Dobson's report here," she said, thumbing through the file. "Here it is. He merely states that three girls spotted the bomb and reported it to you, whereupon you telephoned the police. And yet, we have been told that the girls carried the bomb into the school" she gave an affected shudder, "and that you carried it back out again!"

"May I ask who told you that?" Mrs. Langfeld asked, thinking she would find out at last what she wanted to know.

"We don't know. He didn't give his name. When my secretary asked he replied that he preferred not to say, but felt he ought to let us know, as he was concerned for the safety of the pupils."

"I see," Mrs. Langfeld said thoughtfully, hardly amazed that Mr. Campbell sprang immediately to mind.

"You don't seem surprised," Miss Hall commented, eyeing her searchingly, "and you don't deny it. Does that mean that we were correctly informed?"

The headmistress sighed. "Oh yes," she said, "it's quite correct."

"Then why?"

Interrupting the question, Mrs. Langfeld once again launched into an explanation of her motives. Miss Hall listened attentively, nodding understandingly when she finished.

"Quite right!" she agreed. "I admire your principles. Just what's needed to keep the young girls of today under control! And in my opinion, you did the right thing, running out with that bomb. But what courage it must have taken! Weren't you afraid?"

"Well, yes, I suppose I was. But there wasn't time to think about that. I just wanted to get the thing away from the school as quickly as possible!"

Miss Hall tut-tutted and her look of unmasked admiration caused Mrs. Langfeld to blush with embarrassment. "What bravery!" she whispered with awe. "I think you deserve a medal. I wish I could publish the true story."

"Oh, please don't!" Mrs. Langfeld begged.

"Yes, yes, I understand...and I won't. It's a pity, though. Mrs. Langfeld, now that I'm here, could I have a look round the school? I'm interested to see it."

"With pleasure!" Mrs. Langfeld said, relieved that yet another crisis had been averted.

As Mrs. Langfeld took Miss Hall around she was pleased to find that Miss Hall was not as forbidding and unapproachable as she had seemed at first. They walked from classroom to classroom, and Miss Hall watched lessons in progress. Then Mrs. Langfeld introduced Miss Hall to Miss Zemmel and Mrs. Hoffman. Mrs. Hoffman, of course, insisted on pressing one of her delicious chocolate cakes upon her.

"I must say, I'm impressed!" Miss Hall remarked, when the conducted tour was over. "You run this school impressively well! The girls all look happy and are quite well-behaved, not at all like most of the children I'm used to seeing!" The expression on her face gave the impression that her experience with schoolchildren had not always been enjoyable. "I shall recommend this school strongly from now on and I'll do whatever I can to see that it qualifies for a grant!"

Miss Hall then shook Mrs. Langfeld's hand enthusiastically and left. Mrs. Langfeld, somewhat bemused by this unexpected turn of events, went into her office to gather her thoughts.

She was extremely upset that there was someone about who bore such a resentment against her school that he went out of his way to cause trouble for it, but the way things had turned out this time, she had to admit that this particular cloud had a silver lining! "*Gam zu letovah,*" she said to herself, expressing her gratitude to *Hashem* and resolving not to worry about her unknown enemy.

Her eye fell upon a letter she had received that morning, which had also given her pleasure. It was from Mrs. Laufer, the matron of the Chingford Nursing Home, who had written to thank her for allowing the school choir to begin to come down every month to entertain the ladies at the Home.

"*Everyone enjoys their beautiful singing tremendously,*" she wrote, "*and I'm sure it does my patients a lot of good! I hope they will continue coming, even though Mrs. Horowitz is now ready to leave our home.*"

So, Nechy's mother is leaving, Mrs. Langfeld reflected. She must be a lot better, *Boruch Hashem*! Mrs. Langfeld wondered where Mrs. Horowitz would go and what she would do after the nursing home.

Nechy, meanwhile, had also received a letter from Mrs. Laufer. In Mrs. Laufer's letter, however, she had enclosed a letter from Dr. Sykora. Full of mixed feelings, Nechy immediately sought out Shulamis.

"But that's wonderful!" Shulamis cried, when she had read both letters. "Dr. Sykora thinks she's well enough to leave the nursing home! Oh Nechy, I'm so happy for you!" She hugged her friend enthusiastically. But at the same time she was worried. Would Nechy have to leave the school?

"Yes, I know—and I'm thrilled, really I am! But *how* will she cope? She's all alone! I can't just stay here and leave her to fend for herself, can I?"

"No, I suppose not," Shulamis replied solemnly, her expression suddenly becoming serious. Shulamis knew Nechy did not want to leave school yet—and she could not bear the thought of Nechy leaving. "But I'm sure your mother won't want you to cut your schooling short. And Mrs. Laufer must be making some arrangements for her. She wouldn't just let her leave the nursing home without making sure she's well cared for!"

"I don't know," Nechy sounded doubtful. "She knows she's got me." She sighed. "Oh well, I'll find out what's happening when I go next week, to take her back to London And whatever's decided, I've made up my mind to accept it, without behaving like I did before." She struggled to keep the wistfulness out of her voice.

"Oh, Nechy! You've come such a long way!" Shulamis declared admiringly.

"You're acting so much different than before! I do hope you'll return to school. I'd miss you too much if you didn't!"

Nechy smiled warmly at her. "Don't think I'm going to get too wrapped up in Mummy to abandon you!" she said. "You're going to keep coming to us whenever you can. Mummy likes you, I know she does and I will never ever forget everything you've done for me!"

That Shabbos seemed to last longer than usual for Shulamis, not knowing whether her friend would be coming back or not. Nechy had left on Thursday afternoon to spend Shabbos at Chingford before taking her mother to London on Sunday as arranged. Shulamis had toyed with the idea of asking if she should go with her but she had resisted. She knew Nechy should be alone with her mother.

Nechy had had similar thoughts during those few days before her departure. So many times she had almost blurted out, "Shulamis, ask Mrs. Langfeld if you can come with me. I really need your support!" but she had stopped herself every time. This was something she must face alone. Her mother needed her and she would be no use to her as a coward!

In spite of all her misgivings and worries Nechy was delighted with her mother's progress. She still seemed worn and sad and the nightmares went on, but she looked much better physically and she seemed more like her old self.

She greeted Nechy warmly and began to talk about her plans.

"We're going back to those nice people I stayed with when I came—the Myersons," she told her daughter. "Just till I find a flat for us."

Nechy's face fell. So she *does* want me to stay with her. But immediately Nechy was overcome by a pang of guilt. She must push these thoughts out of her mind!

"And I must also look for a job," Mrs. Horowitz went on.

"Oh Mummy, what for?" Nechy protested in Yiddish, still trying to practice. "You can't start yet! I'll look after you!"

Her mother smiled. "No, Nechy," she said. "I've got to start being a *mensch* again. And anyway, I'm your mother. *I* should be looking after *you!*"

"Of course, Mummy, you will!" Nechy said, hugging her mother. "But I want to help you get your strength back!"

"*Boruch Hashem*. I've got you!" Mrs. Horowitz said with emotion, returning the hug. "Just knowing that gives me *koach!*"

Suddenly Nechy felt that nothing else mattered but her mother's happiness. She would do anything for that!

"What do you think of my Yiddish?" she asked cheerfully.

"It's much better!" her mother declared. "What did you do to improve it?"

"Oh, I practice quite a lot with Shulamis and we both go into the kitchen to chat to Mrs. Hoffman whenever we can."

"Nechy, I really appreciate that you're trying to speak Yiddish!" Mrs. Horowitz said. "At least we'll be able to talk better now.

"And you might learn English." Nechy said without thinking.

"Never!" Mrs. Horowitz exclaimed vehemently, a pained expression crossing her face. "I hate the language! I hate it!"

"Oh Mummy, I'm sorry!" Nechy cried, near to tears, suddenly remembering what Dr. Sykora had told her about the cruel,Nazi officer and his use of English.

But Mrs. Horowitz, regretting her outburst, strove to change the subject quickly. "How is your friend Shulamis?" she asked.

"She's fine," Nechy said. "She sends you her love."

"She's such a nice girl," Mrs. Horowitz commented. "I'm glad she's your friend."

"We've been friends since we were small," Nechy told her.

"Tell me about her. Where is she from? What happened to her family?"

Nechy recounted as much as she knew of Shulamis's history, how her parents had been killed in an accident and how she had been cared for by her grandparents, before being torn away from them and brought to England. Mrs. Horowitz's face clouded over with pity.

"Poor girl," she said, "she's got no one in the world. Yet she's got such a cheerful disposition."

Her mother's words stirred up the old feelings of guilt and shame in Nechy. After all, Shulamis had less to be cheerful about than she had, but she couldn't speak about it to her mother. Maybe one day she would be able to tell her how she had felt, but not yet.

"We'll have to make our home a second home to her," Mrs. Horowitz went on. "She'll be able to come to us for all the holidays…"

Suddenly, Nechy realized how enormously lucky she was. She actually didn't mind any more if she could not go back to school. Even if she had to stay in London it wouldn't be a sacrifice. After all, at long last, she was going to have a home! All her life Nechy had been shuttled from house to house. Always the object of pity and kindness. The orphan. The refugee. Never with her own home. Now she would have a home! A place she could invite others! The idea seemed so exciting.

In that frame of mind she bustled about, organizing her mother's departure from the home. She went into the village on Friday morning to buy some small gifts for the staff, thankful, too, for the small allowance she received every month. She and her mother had a lovely *Shabbos* and then she spent *motzei Shabbos* and last Sunday morning in this depressing place packing Mrs. Horowitz's belongings. In the afternoon they took a train to London, where they were met at Victoria station by Mr. Myerson who took them to his pleasant home in Stamford Hill. They were such kind people, these Myersons. Middle-aged, with their four children married, they had offered their home and hospitality to Mrs. Horowitz—a complete stranger—and made her and her daughter feel like members of the family.

The friendly welcome they received from short, plump Mrs. Myerson gave Nechy a warm feeling and she soon found herself making plans in her mind. Tomorrow she would telephone to make an appointment with Dr. Sykora, who had said she still wanted to continue treating Mrs. Horowitz. Then she would start looking for an apartment of their own. There was so much to do, she could see she would be incredibly busy!

She was taken by surprise, therefore, when her mother casually asked her, "when are you going back to school, Nechy?"

Nechy stared at her. "But I'm not!" she protested. "I'm staying here with you!"

"Don't be silly," Mrs. Horowitz said. "You can't just stop going to school. You've got to finish your studies..."

"But I can go to school in London," Nechy argued.

Her mother shook her head. "I don't want you to change schools now. It wouldn't be good."

Nechy was about to continue the argument but she noticed her mother close her eyes wearily for a moment.

"Mummy, you're tired. You ought to go to bed," she said. "We'll talk about it tomorrow."

Mrs. Horowitz didn't resist when Nechy led her upstairs

to the pleasant, sunny room they shared, gave her her pills and tucked her into bed. Once she was sure her mother was settled, Nechy went downstairs and sought out Mrs. Myerson, intending to ask her advice.

She found their kind-faced, homely hostess in the kitchen, busily washing the large pile of supper dishes. Picking up a tea towel, Nechy began to dry them.

"Mrs. Myerson," she said tentatively, "I don't know what to do. Mummy says I should go back to school, but how can I? She needs me!"

Mrs. Myerson inclined her head slightly, in a thoughtful manner. "I'm sorry. I can't advise you, Nechy. This is something you must make up your own mind about. But if she said so, then..." she broke off, making a vague gesture with her hand.

"But how do I know if it's what she really wants. Maybe she only said it because she thinks it's what I want!"

"And is it what you want?" Mrs. Myerson asked searchingly.

"I don't know," Nechy sounded bewildered. "I want to do what's best for Mummy. How can she cope, after all, on her own?"

"Your mother is tougher than you think. She knows she has to start getting on with life again and she'll cope. And we're all around to keep an eye on her.

"I know, and I'm grateful," Nechy said. "But if I go back to school I'll feel awfully guilty!"

"Nechy," Mrs. Myerson stopped scrubbing an enormous saucepan, and wiping her work-worn hands on her apron, she looked directly at the worried girl. "How do you think your mother will feel if you interrupt your schooling on her account? Won't *she* feel guilty?"

Nechy knew she was probably right. As a result of this

conversation and subsequent ones with her mother, the following Thursday morning, she found herself sitting on the train returning to Elmsleigh. She had stayed on for a few days, hoping to find a flat for her mother, but she soon realized that, in London, this was no easy task and she gave up the search after the Myersons promised to see to it for her.

She was, of course, quite glad she was returning to school and to her friends, even though she could not rid herself of this feeling of concern for her mother. This cloud of worry, she knew, would always be hanging over her.

But, all in all, she told herself, things were definitely looking brighter on the horizon!

HOSTILE
MESSAGES

I T WAS A WARM, SUNNY AFTERNOON AND MRS. Langfeld sat back comfortably in the front seat of the car, feeling utterly relaxed. The Pesach holidays were over and her son, Nochum Tzvi, was driving her back to Elmsleigh. The new term was due to begin the next day but Mrs. Langfeld always went the day before, to prepare everything for her pupils.

She had thoroughly enjoyed the holidays with her family in London. She had intended to give a hand with the Pesach preparations, but her daughter-in-law, Gita, had refused her help, insisting that Mrs. Langfeld take it easy while she had the chance. Knowing that Etty and Bayla, her older daughter, who was home from Gateshead Seminary, were helping with the chores made it easier for Mrs. Langfeld to accept, that is, as long as she could do her share in looking after her grandson, little Moishy, who had become an active little toddler!

One of the things that had given her immense pleasure during her stay in London was having the chance to see

Mrs. Horowitz again. How different she had become from the gaunt, pathetic woman she had seen eight months ago! Mrs. Horowitz seemed so much healthier now and seemed more definite about the future. Mrs. Myerson had persuaded her to postpone her search for a job and a home of her own until after Pesach, explaining that, as long as she stayed with them, she could manage with the allowance she received from the Refugee Chessed Fund. But now she was raring to go. Nechy, too, seemed to have regained her sparkle, although her new responsibility appeared to have made her more grown up.

As Nochum Tzvi's old car rattled its way through the winding lanes of Elmsleigh Mrs. Langfeld felt her excitement rising, as it always did when she returned to school after the holidays. However happy she was with her family in London, at Migdal Binoh school she was absolutely in her element. In spite of all the trials and tribulations, running the school gave her a tremendous sense of fulfillment.

She thought of the previous term and reflected that it had not been a bad term at all. Although the affair of the bomb had been extremely nerve-racking, subsequently things had been considerably quieter. There had been a few headaches, including a nasty epidemic of flu, a girl getting lost on the *Chamisho Oser B'shvat* outing and Mr. Campbell coming over in the middle of their *Purim* festivities, complaining that the noise was causing his wife to have a migraine attack. But, in general, the school had run fairly smoothly. Now she was looking forward to the Summer term, hoping the students would achieve a great deal.

They were chugging slowly up Woodcroft Lane when Mrs. Langfeld spotted the distant figure of Mr. Hoffman emerging from the Lodge, where he and his wife lived, carrying something that looked like a bucket, while Mrs. Hoffman bustled behind him, with what appeared to be a broom in her hand.

"What's going on?" she asked, puzzled. "Can you go a bit faster?"

"Not so easy with this old banger," her son Nochum Tzvi replied, "this lane's rather uphill." Nevertheless, he did increase his speed and they caught up with the Hoffmans at the gate.

"Hello!" Mrs. Langfeld said, getting out of the car. "What's up?" She eyed the bucket, from which a strong smell of turpentine emanated, as well as the article in Mrs. Hoffman's hand, which turned out to be a long-handled scrubbing-brush.

"Yoy, Minna!" Mrs. Hoffman cried, "We didn't want you should see it!" There was consternation in her voice, with its strong Hungarian accent.

"See what?" Mrs. Langfeld queried, following their involuntary gaze toward the gate. What she saw, daubed on the wide brick gateposts, made her gasp in horror!

On the left gatepost, written in large, irregular letters with white paint, were the words: JEWS GET OUT! And the right post bore the message: WE DON'T WANT YOU HERE!

The color drained from Mrs. Langfeld's face as she stared at the words, unable to speak for a moment. Eventually she managed to stammer, "W-when was this done?"

Mrs. Hoffman eyed her with concern. "Yoy, Minna! You look terrible! Come to the Lodge with me and have a sweet tea. Berel will scrub it from the wall!"

"No, thank you, Mrs. Hoffman," Mrs. Langfeld said, sighing wearily. "I want to get inside straight away. But who could have done this? And when?"

"It wasn't there yesterday," Berel Hoffman told her. "I just saw it not long ago, when I went past…"

"Yoy! You should have seen him, Minna!" his wife interrupted, her plump frame shaking vigorously. "As white as a sheet, he was! 'Berel!' I cried, 'what has happened?' But he couldn't even speak at first. Then he told me and I went out to see. Yoy, Minna, it's terrible! It's all happening all over again! Just like before in Germany! Even here we are not safe!" She picked up the end of her starched green apron and held it to her eyes, weeping bitterly into it.

"Mrs. Hoffman," Mrs. Langfeld said gently, putting an arm across the cook's shoulders, "this has been a bigger shock to you than you realize. I think *you* should go to the Lodge and make yourself a cup of sweet tea."

Mrs. Hoffman wiped her eyes and looked up, shaking her head. "No," she protested. "I must help Berel scrub this off!"

"No, Magda," her husband argued. "Do what Mrs. Langfeld tells you. I can manage by myself."

"Yes, Berel, all right," Mrs. Hoffman said, sniffing, "I'll go then." And she scampered off, mumbling, "Yoy! What a shock! What a shock! Just like the Nazis!"

Mr. Hoffman watched her for a moment, a look of concern on his face. Then he dipped the scrubbing-brush into the bucket and advanced with it toward the offensive lettering. The smell of turpentine was so overpowering that Mrs. Langfeld took a step backwards, colliding with Nochum Tzvi, who, in turn, collided with Mr. Campbell, who had just come up behind him.

"Watch out!" Mr. Campbell cried, steadying him. Drawing his bushy eyebrows together, he treated Nochum Tzvi to a penetrating stare for a moment before turning to Mrs. Langfeld. "Ah, good afternoon, Mrs. Langfeld. Is there anything wrong?" he asked, sensing the atmosphere. Before anyone could reply, he looked at Mr. Hoffman, who was about to start scrubbing the words on the gatepost, and gaped.

"Dear me!" he exclaimed, shaking his head and tut-tut-ting. "This is shocking! Who's done this?"

"That is what we would like to know!" Mrs. Langfeld replied tartly.

Mr. Campbell went up to the gatepost and fingered some of the letters. "Gloss paint," he announced factually. "You'll have a difficult job getting it off. Someone must have been determined you would get the message!"

"I just can't imagine anyone in this village doing some-thing like this!" Mrs. Langfeld declared with surprise, shaking her head. "Everyone seems so friendly."

"So they are," Mr. Campbell agreed, though Mrs. Langfeld had an uncomfortable feeling that there was a sneer behind his smile, "but you know what the rural English are like! They really don't like anyone who is different. If you don't mind a piece of friendly advice, Mrs. Langfeld, perhaps if you changed your attitude a little and let your pupils inte-grate you wouldn't face these kind of problems!"

"Yes, Mr. Campbell, you have aired that view before and I'm afraid it is something we will *never* agree on!" Mrs. Langfeld took a large bunch of silver keys out of her leather bag as she spoke and selected one. "Now, if you will excuse me, I would like to unlock the gate so that my son can drive the car in."

"This is your son, is it?" Mr. Campbell remarked with interest, his lips turning down distastefully as he eyed Nochum Tzvi's black beard and *yarmulke*, as well as the *tzitzis* showing under Nochum Tzvi's shirt and jacket. Yet he raised his hat and said politely, "Pleased to meet you, Mr. Langfeld."

Nochum Tzvi returned the greeting with a nod and began to rev up his engine, while his mother swung the gates open. With a shrug, Mr. Campbell pushed his hands into the pockets of his jacket and ambled off down the lane. Nochum Tzvi drove through the gates, waving to Mr. Hoffman, who was busy scrubbing away at the gateposts.

"Who was that man?" Nochum Tzvi asked his mother, getting out of the car at the front door.

"Mr. Campbell? You could call him our next-door-neighbor. He lives in the cottage a bit further down."

"I didn't like the look of him," Nochum Tzvi remarked. "I've a feeling he shares the sentiments of whoever wrote that message. Did you see the way he looked me up and down? I don't think *he's* overly fond of Jews either!"

"Yes," Mrs. Langfeld agreed, "I've sometimes had that feeling too. In his own quiet way, he can be quite a troublemaker, though he's always been polite and gentlemanly to me."

"The typical Englishman," her son commented with a wry smile.

"Actually, he says he's Scottish," Mrs. Langfeld informed him.

"Well, whatever he is, if you have any trouble with him, let me know and I'll come over and deal with him!"

Mrs. Langfeld smiled gratefully at him, even though she knew there was not much he could do. Although he had been a young *yeshiva bochur* when his father was killed, he had immediately displayed a protectiveness toward her that warmed her heart. Now only twenty-five years old, he seemed in many ways more mature than his age, in spite of his boyish smile. How like Aryeh he was! Not only in looks—he was of average height and slim, with that straight-forward, honest look in his hazel-colored eyes—but he had that same way of making her feel secure and cared for.

Together they carried her suitcases into the house and Mrs. Langfeld went straight into the kitchen to make them both a cup of coffee. There she found two cups and saucers prepared on the table and a plate of chocolate cake in the center on a pretty flowered plate.

"Trust Mrs. Hoffman!" she said appreciatively. "Her own special brand of welcome!"

She filled up the kettle and put it on to boil.

"What are you going to do about what's happened?" Nochum Tzvi soon asked, as she poured out their coffee. "Are you going to notify the police?"

"No, I don't think so," his mother said thoughtfully. "After all, no real harm is done. I think it's best to ignore it. I only hope Mr. Hoffman manages to erase the words completely. I wouldn't like the girls to see it—or the staff either. And Miss Zemmel! I shudder to think how she would react, after all she's been through in Germany before the war. In fact, I hope he gets it off quickly, because she is due to arrive here soon. She's spent Pesach with Mrs. Gold in Chesham, and she knows I'll be at the school today."

As if on cue, a key could be heard in the front door lock and a moment later, slamming the door shut loudly, Miss Zemmel rushed in, obviously in a state of distress. Her usually impeccable appearance was somewhat disturbed. Even her normally crisp navy uniform seemed slightly ruffled and her grey hair, pulled back in a bun, had loosened a little.

"*Schrecklich! Schrecklich!*" the matron cried, wringing her hands. "Ach, Mrs. Langfeld, it is terrible! I never thought that in England such a thing can happen!" She sank onto a chair and covered her face with her hands.

"Miss Zemmel, *please* calm down," Mrs. Langfeld said. "First of all, *Shalom Aleichem!* Did you have a nice—"

"Ach! *Shalom Aleichem! Shalom Aleichem!*" Miss Zemmel repeated sarcastically, interrupting her. "Ja, Ja! You can say that now, but soon will come a time when we will be afraid such words to say!"

"Miss Zemmel, what are you so worked up about?" Mrs. Langfeld asked. "If it's because of those words on the wall—"

"Ja! It is! I *saw* what was written! Some of it Mr. Hoffman washed off, but he told me what it was…and the rest I saw!" Miss Zemmel sighed deeply. "So it started in Germany," she said with immense sadness, "and now here as well." She sank into a chair and covered her face with her hands, trembling with agitation. She was not the sort to cry and so she just sat in the chair trembling and agitated.

Over a cup of coffee, Mrs. Langfeld and Nochum Tzvi tried their best to reassure her and calm her down—although Mrs. Langfeld understood Miss Zemmel only too well, knowing what the matron had suffered before escaping from Berlin and coming to England. Mrs. Langfeld had heard enough about the way the Nazis had persecuted the Jews, even though she herself had come here before it had all begun. Eventually they managed to persuade Miss Zemmel that she had nothing to worry about.

"Maybe you are right," the matron said, sounding much calmer, if not entirely convinced. "So! Now upstairs I must go to see if everything is in order."

Mrs. Langfeld stood up too, announcing that she had a lot to see to before the girls arrived the next day.

"Well, I'll make my way back to London," Nochum Tzvi said, picking up his car keys. "Bye, Mum, and please take care! Don't work too hard!"

"Don't worry," his mother replied, "and Nochum Tzvi, *please* don't tell Etty about all this. It's better if the girls know nothing about it."

"Yes, you're right. But I hope it doesn't happen again!"

"Oh, I'm sure it won't!" Mrs. Langfeld said confidently. "It was probably some young hooligan with nothing better to do, making the most of the fact that we were away."

Although Mrs. Langfeld had been badly shaken at the time, once Mr. Hoffman had removed all traces of the abusive daubing she convinced herself that it was an isolated incident and would not occur again.

As the school settled down for another term, there was so much she had to do that the unpleasant affair almost faded from her mind.

The shock was all the greater, therefore, when Mrs. Gold, the English and History teacher, who did not stay at the school, but commuted every day from her home in nearby Chesham, came rushing in one morning, extremely agitated.

"Minna," she cried breathlessly, bursting into the office, "I've just seen something terrible!"

"Leah! You look dreadful!" Mrs. Langfeld cried, staring aghast at the teacher's pale face. "What has happened?"

"I always get off the bus near the local village primary school," Mrs. Gold told her, "and as I passed the school I was shocked when I saw something written in paint on the outside wall! Such a horrible message!" Mrs. Gold was shaking her head, visibly upset.

"Oh no! Not again!" Mrs. Langfeld said, almost inaudibly, looking down at her shoes. She had hoped that they had put this behind them.

"What do you mean, *again*?" Mrs. Gold asked, puzzled, taking off her horn-rimmed spectacles, which had become steamed up, and patting her light-brown sheitel back into place, as she stared at Mrs. Langfeld.

"I'll tell you in a minute," the headmistress said, "but please tell me, what was written there?"

"It said…" Mrs. Gold took a deep breath, bracing herself, "It said…GO AWAY, JEWS. WE DON'T WANT YOU IN OUR VILLAGE…!"

"I see," Mrs. Langfeld said thoughtfully. Then she told Mrs. Gold what had happened the day before school had begun. "I think I had better pay a call on Mrs. Lomas, the headmistress of the school!"

THE LANGFELDS
INVESTIGATE

"**I** CAN'T TELL YOU HOW BAD I FEEL ABOUT THIS, Mrs. Langfeld!" Mrs. Lomas said, looking at her visitor with concern in her candid, gray-blue eyes. "It upsets me to know that my school should have been used for such an unpleasant piece of work!"

Mrs. Langfeld had met the headmistress of Elmsleigh Village School before, when they had both attended a meeting of teachers at the Town Hall, but she had never actually spoken to her. Now she regarded her with interest and liked what she saw. Slender and quite petite, Mrs. Lomas looked to be in her fifties. She had graying, auburn hair which was swept into a bun at the nape of her neck, framing an oval face with finely-cut features. Her bearing was gentle, yet authoritative, inspiring trust in the people who spoke to her. She wore a pretty grey suit with ruffled sleeves.

"But why should you feel bad?" Mrs. Langfeld protested. "It's not *your* fault that someone chose the wall of your school. I'm sure your pupils had nothing to do with it."

"No, I can reassure you on that point. I have been into all the classrooms and questioned the children and believe me, I can tell when they are telling the truth—and when they are not."

Mrs. Langfeld nodded. "The thing to do now is to remove the writing from the wall as quickly as possible," she said.

"Yes, I can understand how you feel," Mrs. Lomas agreed sympathetically, "and I would have told the caretaker to do it straight away, but I thought you might want to leave it for the police to see."

"Oh, I don't know if I want to involve the police," Mrs. Langfeld said doubtfully. "The less fuss that's made the better."

"I don't agree. I think the police should be told, so that they put a stop to it." Mrs. Lomas leaned forward and eyed the other headmistress directly. "Mrs. Langfeld, I'm sure I can speak openly to you. The fact is, although I'm *sure* none of my pupils are responsible for this deed, it has already had an effect on some of them. One or two of the younger ones were overheard to make some…well, to put it bluntly…some anti-Semitic remarks, which has never occurred in this school before. Of course, my staff and I hastened to nip it in the bud. We explained to the children how wrong such feelings are and how we must welcome the Jewish people in our midst and do our best to make up for the suffering the Germans inflicted on them." She looked anxiously at Mrs. Langfeld, hoping her words had not caused her pain. But Mrs. Langfeld nodded, appreciating her frankness.

"Obviously the person who did this is trying to incite anti-Semitism in this village. Surely that is all the more reason why we should get it off the wall immediately," she argued, quite convincingly. "We had a similar slogan painted on our school and we removed it before many people saw it. As it is, it caused a lot of distress to our matron and the cook, who have both suffered in the war."

"Perhaps you are right then," Mrs. Lomas said, sympathy written on her face. "But I still think you should notify the police. We can always tell them what had been written. They'll surely believe us."

"Maybe you're right," Mrs. Langfeld was thoughtful for a few moments. "I *would* like to make sure this thing is stopped—and I would also like to know who is doing it. Mrs. Lomas, do you think there is a general dislike of Jews here in this village? Because, if there is, I will have to move the school elsewhere. I have a few war orphans amongst my pupils, as well as members of the staff, as I told you, who have suffered enough. I wouldn't want to subject them to any more."

"Oh, it would be a shame if you moved away!" Mrs. Lomas cried. "I don't think you have any cause to worry about anti-Semitism here. I, myself, have never come across it. But then, I don't actually live in the village. I come in from High Wycombe every day."

"I see," Mrs. Langfeld stood up. "Well, I shall ask a few locals that I know. Thank you so much for your time and all your help, Mrs. Lomas. You've been so helpful. And you know, you've convinced me and I shall take your advice and get in touch with the police.

Superintendent Blake, a rather large man with rugged features and unruly straw-colored hair, took a puff at his pipe and shook his head ruefully. He was well acquainted with Mrs. Langfeld, having dealt with a case of kidnapping at the school the previous year. He had a high regard for the head-mistress, which was why he was interesting himself in this case, instead of delegating it to one of his subordinates. But now he would have to tell her that she had made a stupid mistake.

"I'm afraid I can't help you," he said, "not having seen the actual daubing. You should have left them for my men to scrutinize. Even then, it would have been hard to find the culprit. But now," he spread his hand out in a helpless gesture, "we have nothing to go by at all!"

"But I told you why I wanted them removed!" Mrs. Langfeld protested.

"Yes, and I understand. But the fact remains that you have removed all the evidence."

Mrs. Langfeld stood up, a look of disappointment and frustration on her face.

"Does that mean you won't take any action at all?" she asked anxiously.

Superintendent Blake nodded. "Unfortunately there is nothing we can do at this stage," he said. "If it happens again please leave things as they are and contact us immediately."

"I sincerely hope it won't happen again!" Mrs. Langfeld declared. "Twice was enough! Well, thank you for sparing the time, Superintendent. Good afternoon." She began to walk toward the door.

"I'm sorry I couldn't help you," Blake called after her as she went out.

Mrs. Langfeld nodded to the two police sergeants at the main desk as she passed, her head held high. But as soon as she was outside the police station her shoulders seemed to droop.

She felt she had come to a dead end. The police could do nothing unless the offender struck again, yet the last thing she wanted was to have another nasty slogan painted on a wall in a public place, left there for all to see! Where, then, did that leave her?

She could not rid herself of the feeling that it was Mr. Campbell who was responsible, even though he had expressed amazement on seeing the words on the school gateposts. Had he really been as surprised as he had made out? How would she ever know? In all her dealings in this town, he was the only one who seemed clearly antagonistic towards Jews. She remembered vividly how he had eyed Nochum Tzvi with such obvious distaste.

But maybe she was wrong. It was just a feeling after all. She had no proof. Well, there was nothing more she could do. Now she must concern herself with the other aspect of the affair that was worrying her—the possibility of anti-Semitic feelings at large in the village. The first person she questioned was Mrs. Payne, the school cleaner.

"No! 'Course there ain't!" Mrs. Payne declared emphatically. "Well, not so as I've noticed, anyway. None of my friends or neighbors as ever said anything unkind about the Jews…well, they'd 'ave 'ad me to reckon with if they 'ad! But I tell you what. If you really wants to know what goes on in the village ask Mrs. 'Uxley, the postmistress, down at the post office. What she don't know about this village ain't worth knowing!"

Taking her advice, Mrs. Langfeld sauntered casually into the small post office, early next morning and asked for a book of stamps. The post office was empty except for Mrs. Huxley behind the counter—a tall, angular woman with sparse grey hair and a wrinkled, weather-beaten face. Mrs. Langfeld began to search around in her mind for a way to steer the conversation round to the subject she wanted, when the postmistress herself provided an opening.

"'Morning!" she said cheerfully. "Lovely day, isn't it!"

"Yes, so it is," Mrs. Langfeld agreed.

"Well, it was a beautiful day yesterday too, not a cloud in

the sky!" Mrs. Huxley went on, "but I bet you didn't feel so cheerful then, after what happened!"

Mrs. Langfeld smiled. The great thing about a small town was the speed with which news traveled. "I don't feel too happy about it now either," Mrs. Langfeld retorted, "In fact, I won't until we find out who did it!"

"Mmm," the postmistress murmured sympathetically, "must have been some young ruffian—or a lunatic."

"Maybe..." Mrs. Langfeld sounded doubtful. "Mrs. Huxley," she said suddenly, seizing her opportunity, "would you say that what was written there reflects the general feeling of the people round here?"

"You mean anti-racial feelings? No, I wouldn't say so. No one I know seems to have anything against the Jewish people. Most of them are shocked at what happened during the war and what the Nazis did to them! And I, for one, am quite impressed by you and your school. Your girls always seem polite and well-mannered when they come in here. It must be the way you educate them!"

"We try our best," Mrs. Langfeld murmured, embarrassed, but gratified by her praise.

"And what's more," the postmistress continued with enthusiasm, "I'm going to ask the next person who comes in and I'm sure they'll say the same!"

Almost as if it had been waiting for a cue, the door to the post office gave its friendly 'PING' and opened to admit another customer. Mrs. Langfeld turned round and saw, to her horror, that it was none other than Mr. Campbell! She couldn't believe the coincidence. Desperate to prevent Mrs. Huxley from mentioning the subject to him, she snatched up her stamps, thrusting the money behind the grill, saying hastily, "Excuse me. I must hurry up! I'm late!"

But before Mrs. Langfeld could leave, Mrs. Huxley said,

"Mr. Campbell, help me put Mrs. Langfeld's mind at rest. Am I not right in saying that there are no anti-Jewish feelings in this village?"

Mrs. Langfeld looked at Mr. Campbell. Did she imagine it, Mrs. Langfeld wondered, or was there a slight tightening of Mr. Campbell's face muscles? However, he answered with perfect equanimity.

"I'm hardly the right person to ask," he said slowly, "being a comparative stranger here in Elmsleigh. But I'm sure you are right. I, myself, have certainly never come across any. Why are you so worried, Mrs. Langfeld?" he asked, turning to her.

"I think I have reason to be. You've seen the message that was written on our school gateposts, haven't you?"

"Yes, but that was an isolated incident. Nothing to be alarmed about!"

"I'm afraid you're wrong," the headmistress told him. "There was another one yesterday."

"Is that so?" Mr. Campbell stared at her for a moment. Then he shrugged. "All the same, it's nothing to get worked up about. If you ask me, it's just some young maniac with a chip on his shoulder. I wouldn't be surprised if it's someone who felt he'd been badly treated at school, seeing that he chose school walls to daub on."

Mrs. Langfeld's eyes narrowed. "How do you know the second one was also on a school wall," she asked, eyeing him shrewdly.

Mr. Campbell looked put out for a moment. Then, collecting himself, he replied, "Now that you have come to mention it, I do remember hearing about it."

He was lying, of course, but how could she prove it? How stupid she had been to ask him that question. It had put him on his guard and even if the police were to question him he would easily bluff his way out of it.

Utterly frustrated, she bid them a hasty goodbye and hurried out of the post office. She was now quite convinced of Mr. Campbell's guilt, but couldn't guess why he was doing it. Until now his complaints and objections had, perhaps, made sense in a way. But this latest act was beyond comprehension! Was he just insane with an axe to grind—or did he have some other ulterior motive. Perhaps someone was paying him to edge the school out of the premises so that they could acquire them. Whatever it was, his presence spelled trouble for the school and she could see no way of getting him off their backs. The only way she would ever be able to convince the police was to catch Mr. Campbell red-handed—and she had a feeling, somehow, that if he had written nasty things on walls he would not use that line of attack again!

"Mummy, are you all right?" Etty poked her head round the door of Mrs. Langfeld's room, eyeing her mother anxiously. She had rarely seen her mother looking so tense and nervous.

"Yes, of course I am," Mrs. Langfeld replied, not very convincingly. "Come on in."

Although Mrs. Langfeld tried hard not to differentiate in public too much between her daughter and the other girls at the school, there was one privilege she did allow her. Every night, before going to bed, Etty would come and bid her mother goodnight, often indulging in a little chat at the same time. Etty usually found her mother in her office, still hard at work, but tonight she found the office door locked, and that, coupled with the fact that her mother had been looking rather worried lately, caused Etty some concern. She raced upstairs to Mrs. Langfeld's room and knocked, a little impatiently, at the door, opening it as soon as she heard her mother's reply.

"You're worried about something," she said directly, flopping down on the neatly-made bed, "and I wish you would tell me what it is!"

"It's nothing you need worry your head about," Mrs. Langfeld replied, ruffling her daughter's light brown hair fondly.

"But it is *something*!" Etty cried, almost triumphantly, "and I want to know what!"

Mrs. Langfeld sighed, suddenly tired of all this hedging and being secretive.

"I hadn't really intended to tell you…and I certainly don't want the other girls to know," she said, "but yes, you're right. Something has upset me."

She told Etty all that had happened and the girl's hazel eyes opened wide as she gaped at her mother, horror written all over her heart-shaped face.

"How awful!" she exclaimed. "No wonder you're so upset! Whoever could have done such a thing?"

"I wish I knew!" Mrs. Langfeld sighed. "Unfortunately, the police can't do anything because both times we scrubbed off the evidence."

"I bet it was Mr. Campbell!" Etty announced, to her mother's surprise.

"What makes you say that?" she asked sharply.

Etty shrugged. "I don't know. I just have a funny feeling about him. There's something odd and underhand about him, if you ask me."

Although Etty was just echoing her own sentiments, Mrs. Langfeld knew she could not encourage her to make wild accusations.

"Etty!" she said sternly, "you can't just make statements like that about people! You have absolutely *nothing* to go by!"

"But Mummy, he's forever causing trouble and complaining!" Etty protested.

"Maybe, but he's always been perfectly civil. And if you go round casting aspersions about him—or anyone else—you could get yourself into a load of trouble!"

Etty said no more, but privately resolved to do a bit of sleuthing by herself. Somehow, she *must* remove the worried frown from her mother's forehead by finding some evidence that would reveal the culprit. Her mother had had enough trouble this year.

But where should Etty begin? For a few days she wandered about, frustrated because she did not know how to begin her investigation. Her first break came on *Lag B'omer.*

It was a warm, sunny day and pupils and teachers alike, including Mrs. Langfeld, piled into the two buses that had been hired to take them on an outing to a beautiful spot in a nearby village. As Etty was about to climb onto the bus she noticed Mr. Campbell watching them from a little further down the lane.

It suddenly occurred to her that, if he were the one, he surely would take the opportunity to daub another ugly slogan on the wall, thinking that the place was deserted.

Acting on an impulse, she went up to Mrs. Langfeld, who was busy organizing the girls in their seats, and, tapping her elbow, she said, "Mummy, do you mind if I don't go with everyone on the outing? I've got an awful headache! And I feel as if my hay fever is starting up again!"

Mrs. Langfeld regarded her daughter with alarm. Never before had she known Etty to allow her hay fever to stand in the way of enjoyment. She really must be feeling bad, she thought, if she's willing to miss an outing!

"Oh dear," she said with concern, scrutinizing Etty's face, which was screwed up in pain, even though she did not look pale. "You'd better stay here then. I won't go either."

"Oh no!" Etty cried, suddenly feeling terribly guilty. "You must go! I'll be upset if you don't! I'm not terribly ill or any-thing—and I'm *not* a baby! Besides, Miss Zemmel is here and so is Mrs. Hoffman, so I'm not alone."

Reluctantly, Mrs. Langfeld agreed to go, telling herself that she must stop treating Etty like an baby, but it was with a heavy heart that she watched her daughter get off the bus. It was all so unlike Etty that she could not help worrying.

Etty watched the two busses full of girls drive away and was suddenly overcome with a pang of regret. Hadn't she been a bit too hasty? After all, she could have raced back inside and told Miss Zemmel or Mrs. Hoffman to keep a look-out. But then she remembered what her mother had told her about the way they had both reacted and she decid-ed she had done the right thing after all.

Miss Zemmel fussed over her a bit, trying to persuade her to go and lie down, which was the last thing she wanted to do. That would really have defeated her plan! She waited half-an-hour before announcing that she felt much better and would spend most of the day outdoors to take advantage of the warm and sunny weather.

She sat outside on the lawn with a book, but from time to time she crept furtively up to the gate and peeped out.

There was no sign of Mr. Campbell, or anyone else, for that matter and she soon realized, to her disappointment and chagrin, that the spiteful graffiti-writer was not coming and that she had missed a fabulous outing for nothing!

A few days later, however, Etty's efforts were finally rewarded!

She was taking a stroll with Reisy, who was beginning to wonder why her friend had suddenly developed a passion for walking up and down Woodcroft Lane, when she saw Mr. Campbell come out of his house with a brown paper bag in his hand and go toward the communal refuse-bin in the street. Quickly, she pulled Reisy behind a tree.

"Shh!" she whispered urgently, before Reisy could protest or demand an explanation, "I don't want him to see us!"

"But why?" Reisy wanted to know.

"I can't explain just yet. But it's quite important!"

They peeped furtively round the tree and watched Mr. Campbell lift the lid of the bin and throw the bulky-looking paper bag inside. When she was quite sure he was back inside his house, Etty crept surreptitiously up to the bin, with Reisy behind her.

"Etty! What on earth are you doing?" Reisy asked nervously, still whispering, as her friend lifted the lid, sniffing in disgust at the smell of rotting food, and took out the paper bag. Holding the bag gingerly, she peeped inside, ignoring Reisy's question. What she saw made her practically dance with excitement. The bag contained an almost empty tin of white gloss paint and a small paint brush!

"Wow!" she exclaimed in an awed whisper. Then, seeing the perplexed expression on Reisy's face, she said, "Oh Reisy! It's not fair! I really must explain it all to you, even though Mummy didn't want me to tell anyone. But I know I can trust you with a secret. So come on, I'll tell you on the way because I've got to get this to Mummy straight away. I know she'll be awfully interested to see it!"

Superintendent Blake leaned back in his chair, his expression skeptical as he looked at the objects on his desk.

"It's nothing much to go on," he commented.

"But it seems the right kind of paint," Mrs. Langfeld insisted, her tone desperate. "And the paintbrush looks the same thickness!"

"That may be so, but it's hardly conclusive. Hundreds of people could use the same paint and the same sized brush."

"Well, why can't you search his house and see if he's been doing some decorating? If he hasn't that should be enough proof!"

"Mrs. Langfeld," the Superintendent's tone was patronizing, "I think you're making a mistake. Mr. Campbell may be new to the district, but he seems to have become quite influential. I hear he will be standing for the council elections. If it becomes known that you suspected him of an offense and he proves his innocence, it could make things quite awkward for you. Take my advice, Mrs. Langfeld," he went on in a more kindly tone, "and drop the whole matter. I wouldn't like to see your excellent school in trouble!"

Mrs. Langfeld left the police station in a despondent mood. Her hands were tied, she realized. And now Mr. Campbell was standing for a seat on the council. If he were to be elected he was sure to make things more difficult than ever for her and for the school!

MOUNTING PRESSURE

I N THE DAYS THAT FOLLOWED LITTLE WAS SEEN of Mr. Campbell, much to Mrs. Langfeld's relief. As she expected, no more anti-Semitic slogans appeared in the village, which only strengthened her conviction that he was the culprit.

However, much as she would have liked to push thoughts of her troublesome neighbor out of her mind, there were constant reminders of him all over the village. Large posters, featuring a big photograph of Mr. Campbell, smiling smugly, were displayed on walls and windows, inviting people to 'VOTE FOR CAMPBELL.' Leaflets from all the candidates were pushed through the front door of the school even though no one there was eligible to vote, Mrs. Langfeld's official residential address being in London, as were those of most of the staff.

Picking up the leaflet of the Liberal Party, which was the one Mr. Campbell represented, Mrs. Langfeld found herself scanning it against her will. She felt nauseated as she read a list of the man's "virtues." It praised the interest he had shown in village affairs, especially in the field of education, in the short time he had lived there and told the electors how he was planning to improve the school system, if elected. That was enough to fill Mrs. Langfeld with apprehension.

Still, she told herself hopefully, he might not get in! She crumpled up the leaflet and threw it away, resolving not to think about it, and get on with keeping the school running smoothly!

She succeeded in doing so for a week or so, until the problem reared its ugly head again, with the "Problem of the Sprained Ankle!"

It was the Sunday after *Shevuos*. Most of the girls were spending the afternoon outdoors, drawn out by the warm sunshine, engaging in various outdoor activities. Having spent a pleasant *Yom Tov*, free of lessons, some girls were sitting on the lawn or the wooden garden benches, seriously studying for the forthcoming exams. Other girls were taking things leisurely, reading, playing games or merely sitting around and chatting; and still others left the school grounds to stroll about the village, which they were free to do provided they were back by five o'clock.

Three second-formers, Esty Hyman, Nechama Lieder and Naomi Schiff, however, had miscalculated the time and, realizing they were late, began to hurry back to school. As they were racing up the lane, one of the girls, Nechama, tripped on a stone and fell to the ground with a yelp of pain. The other two bent over her solicitously.

"Are you all right?" Esty asked anxiously.

"No!" Nechama wailed, sitting up and clutching her foot.

"My ankle hurts like mad! I hope it's not broken!" Her small, oval-shaped face looked pinched and her blue eyes were filled with pain.

"Oh no!" Naomi Schiff exclaimed, aghast. "Do you think it is? See if you can stand on it."

"I daren't!" Nechama cried, panic in her voice, "I'm too scared to!" She peered down at her foot and gasped. "Look at it! It's already swollen!"

"Yes, it is!" Naomi agreed, pushing her chestnut hair away from her eyes as she looked at Nechama's ankle, aghast. "What are we going to do? You can't just go on sitting there, waiting for someone to come along and help. We've *got* to get you back to school. If you lean on us and hop, we might manage." The most practical of the three girls, it was quite like her to take charge.

Her tone was coaxing and Nechama allowed them to haul her up, emitting many an "ooh!" and "ah!" as they did so. With her arms across the shoulders of both girls, Nechama hopped forward for a few steps, then, sagging a little, she shook her head. Her fair hair clung to her forehead, which was damp with perspiration.

"It's no use," she said, panting breathlessly, "I'll never make it all the way up there! My ankle hurts *too much!*"

Her friends eyed her with consternation and began to look round for a suitable place for her to sit down when Esty realized they were nearer the gate of the Campbells' cottage than they were to the school grounds.

"Let's take her in there," she suggested. "Maybe they can help."

"No, I don't think we should," Naomi said cautiously. "Mrs. Langfeld always tells us not to go into the houses of strangers."

"But they're not strangers!" Esty declared, her long plaits

swinging emphatically as she argued. "We know who they are. I've seen Mrs. Langfeld talking to him sometimes—and when they moved in I heard they even came to visit her!"

"She's right," Nechama took up the argument, "and anyway, we've got to do something. I can't just stand here in agony!"

Overpowered, Naomi gave in. The three girls made their difficult way slowly up the path, with Nechama wincing with pain every time her foot accidentally touched the ground. Eventually they reached the front door and rang the bell.

It took quite a while for Mrs. Campbell to come to the door. When she did, her hands were wet and soapy and she wiped them dry in the faded floral overall she was wearing. Her eyes flew open in surprise at the sight of two girls holding a third girl between them, who looked on the verge of collapse, with one foot raised.

"Hello?" she said, a question in her voice. "What's happened?"

The girls explained quickly, shifting about uncomfortably as they spoke. In spite of her slight build, Nechama was beginning to weigh heavily on their arms.

"Well, you've come to the right place!" Mrs. Campbell told them with an insipid smile. "I've done an intensive first-aid course, and I even did a bit of nursing when I was young. Come inside and let me have a look at your ankle."

She led the way into the sitting-room and pulled up a chair, signaling to the girls to sit Nechama down on it. Waving her hand toward two more chairs for Esty and Naomi, she drew one up for herself opposite Nechama and began to examine her ankle.

"No, it's not broken," she announced after a few moments. "It's just a bad sprain. I'll put a cold compress on it while I look for a bandage."

She went out of the room and while she was out the girls took a good look round the room, thinking how envious their classmates would be when they told them that they had actually *seen* the inside of the mysterious cottage! It was not a cheerful room. The furniture was dark and solid-looking and the curtains were a heavy dark blue velvet. The thing that struck the girls most was the total lack of ornaments and photographs. There was nothing to tell one what sort of people the occupants were.

Mrs. Campbell soon returned with a first-aid box in one hand, and a large, wet piece of gauze in the other hand.

Nechama expressed her relief as soon as the cold, wet gauze was applied to her ankle and Mrs. Campbell treated her to another wan smile before starting to rummage in the box for a bandage that was the right size.

"Ah, this should do it," she said and, removing the gauze, sat down and deftly wound the bandage round Nechama's foot.

"How does that feel?" Mrs. Campbell asked hopefully.

"Much better!" Nechama declared, preparing to rise from her seat. Mrs. Campbell quickly held out a restricting hand.

"No, don't get up by yourself," she said. "You won't be able to put your foot down for a day or two, but at least you won't be in so much pain while your friends help you hop back to school."

"Thank you so much!" Nechama declared, her words being immediately echoed by the other two.

"Glad I could help," Mrs. Campbell said. "And now I'd like you to do me a favor."

The girls nodded eagerly, glad they could show their appreciation.

"Well, just wait here a minute," Mrs. Campbell said and hurried out. She returned a few minutes later with a plate of cake in her hand.

"I got the recipe from your Mrs. Hoffman," she told them, "and I've just tried it out. I know it can't be as good as hers but I want you to taste it and tell me if it's nearly as good, at least."

The faces of the three girls fell. What on earth were they going to do now? How *could* they refuse the cake without offending Mrs. Campbell? But refuse it they must and it would be best to be open and honest about it.

Nechama took the initiative. "It looks really delicious, really it does! Just like Mrs. Hoffman's! But the trouble is, we're not allowed to have it."

"Not allowed? Whyever not?"

"Because it's not kosher," Esty explained.

"Of course it is!" Mrs. Campbell protested. "I told you, it's Mrs. Hoffman's recipe—and she wouldn't use ingredients that aren't kosher! So there's no reason why you shouldn't have it. And I don't mind telling you, I'll be quite offended if you don't!" She glanced at Nechama's foot, as if to remind them that they had an obligation to her.

The girls had no idea how to explain the situation to her. All they could do was shrug and shake their heads. They were so engrossed in their dilemma that they did not hear Mr. Campbell enter the house.

"What's going on here?" he bellowed from the doorway, startling them.

"Oh Gerald!" Mrs. Campbell cried, her voice tearful, "they refuse to taste my cake!"

"Oh they do, do they?" her husband's tone was menacing. "What are they doing here, in any case?" he asked.

With the injured expression still in her voice, Mrs. Campbell explained about the sprained ankle, telling him how she had bandaged it up…and how they would not even do her a favor and sample her cake.

Mr. Campbell's eyes narrowed as he listened. Then he turned and spoke angrily to the girls. "How dare you insult my wife, after all she's done for you! You will taste that cake, whether you like it or not!"

"B-but we can't! We mustn't…!" Naomi stammered.

"Who says so?" Mr. Campbell demanded fiercely.

"We just know we shouldn't," Nechama replied, her big eyes widening in terror.

"It's what we've always been taught…"

"Aha! So that's what your headmistress is teaching you," he shouted "to insult people who help you! Well, we'll soon put a stop to it! You had better go now. I will not have anyone offending my wife in my house!"

He made a gesture with his hands, as if he were shooing them out. Hastily, Esty and Naomi grabbed hold of Nechama and made for the door. Nechama, hopping painfully along between them, was as anxious as they were to get out of that house as quickly as possible! What a scary man!

"Where on earth have you been?" Mrs. Langfeld cried, meeting the girls at the door when they finally arrived at the school. "You've had us all worried! Don't you realize it's six o'clock?" Her eye fell on Nechama's bandaged foot, and concern immediately replaced her anger. "What happened?" she asked.

The girls gave her an account of most of what had occurred, aware that there was quite a crowd of girls, as well as some staff members, standing around, listening intently. Obviously their absence had caused a good deal of alarm at the school. However, in their recounting, they left out the awkward situation with the cake.

"I see," the headmistress said, when they finished. "Well, you should at least have telephoned from the house to let me know. I've been extremely worried!" She cast another anxious glance at Nechama's foot. "Is it very painful?" she asked sympathetically. "We'd better get the doctor to have a look at it. Miss Zemmel," she turned to the matron who was standing close by, "will you take her up to the sick room? I'll send someone up with some tea and biscuits."

Miss Zemmel took Nechama by the arm and, together with Miss Hertzman, who was also in the hall, helped her up the stairs. Mrs. Langfeld turned to Esty and Naomi.

"I hope you all thanked Mrs. Campbell properly," she said.

The girls nodded, but they could not help blushing, reluctant to tell the headmistress what had happened with the cake. Mrs. Langfeld eyed them quizzically, but dismissed them, resolving to telephone Mrs. Campbell herself to thank her, as soon as she had called the doctor.

To her consternation, it was Mr. Campbell who answered. When she asked to speak to his wife he replied with a curt, "What for?"

"I just want to thank her for what she did."

"Uhuh?" the expression was loaded with sarcasm. "Well, I don't think my wife wants to speak to you. She's still upset over the rudeness of your pupils!"

"I beg your pardon?" There was incredulity in Mrs. Langfeld's voice. However mischievous the younger girls might be, she could not imagine *any* of them being rude to outsiders, especially one that had done them a good turn. And yet...they had blushed when she had questioned them.

"What exactly did they say?" she asked defensively.

"It wasn't what they *said* so much as what they *did*—or rather—didn't do! Emily offered them some cake that she'd baked, in fact, she begged them to taste it because she wanted to know if it was as good as the one your cook bakes, and they had the cheek to refuse! She's extremely hurt, I can tell you!"

Oh, so that was it! Now I understand! Mrs. Langfeld thought. "But Mr. Campbell," she argued, "they never meant to hurt your wife's feelings. They would have gladly tasted the cake if they'd been allowed to! But they weren't allowed to because of Jewish dietary laws."

"Surely they could have made an exception just once," Mr. Campbell argued loftily. Then his tone changed. "Mrs. Langfeld," he went on, adopting a more friendly manner, "I know you think I'm being patronizing, but honestly, I'm telling you this for your own good. You will have to make some changes in your attitude if you want your school to succeed! You must encourage your pupils to conform more with the outside world and join in with the activities of their surroundings. As you know, I hope to be elected on to the council in two weeks and if I'm successful I shall see that some changes are made! You see—

"Yes, thank you, Mr. Campbell," Mrs. Langfeld interrupted abruptly. She had no wish to continue talking to him, fearing she might explode. "The doctor will be here soon. Please thank Mrs. Campbell again for her help."

Before he could reply she hung up. So, she told herself, sighing deeply, that is the way the wind blows. Mr. Campbell was stepping up his campaign and would seize every opportunity to press his point home. Fortunately, these three girls had had the sense to avoid being pressured, but then, the issue had been a simple, straightforward one. They just knew they must not eat unkosher food, and that was that. Another time it might be something more subtle—and might involve first-formers, who were younger and sometimes more gullible. Who knew what danger her pupils might be in!

There was only one thing to be done. Until now she had

pushed that thought out of her mind, not wanting to accept it, but she could evade it no longer and it filled her with an immense sadness. She would have to move her school away from the area—and that meant away from this house for which she had developed a sentimental attachment. A cloud of gloom descended upon her and hung over her for the rest of the week, puzzling everyone around her, as she had decided to tell no one of her decision for the time being. Only Etty questioned her, but gave up when her persistent probing drew no response.

Mrs. Langfeld's spirits soon lifted. Her thoughts were in London where she was waiting for news from her son. It was the following Monday, when she received a telephone call from Nochum Tzvi, telling her the happy news. His wife, Gita, had given birth to a baby boy. Overjoyed, she hurried to tell Etty and the news soon spread like wildfire round the school. The relief at seeing the hitherto glum face of their headmistress wreathed in smiles made the *Mazal Tov* wishes of the pupils and staff all the more fervent.

The next few days were so hectic for Mrs. Langfeld that her problem was pushed to the back of her mind. Besides making two trips into Aylesbury to shop for her new grandson and his older brother, she had to make arrangements for the school to go on running smoothly while she was in London for the *bris*.

When, at last, she sank, exhausted, into her seat on the train on Friday morning, her only feeling was one excitement about the *simchah* ahead, and she leaned back and closed her eyes, basking in happy anticipation!

The baby let out a plaintive yell as Gita's older brother,

who was the *mohel*, performed the *bris* but he was soon placated by the drops of wine placed on his lips. Mrs. Langfeld, standing outside the door with the other women of the family, was overwhelmed by a feeling of protectiveness toward the child.

Nochum Tzvi had told her, just before the *bris*, that he was calling the baby Aryeh, after his father, her late husband, with the additional name Chaim, because Aryeh had died young and under tragic circumstances. Now, as she heard the *Rav* call out the name, *Chaim Aryeh ben Nochum Tzvi*, she felt tears rush to her eyes. Embarrassed, she stole a glance at Gita's mother, Mrs. Kernstein, and, meeting her eyes, saw sympathy and understanding in them. Then she remembered that the other woman had reacted similarly at Moishy's *bris*, since Nochum Tzvi's first son had been named after Gita's father.

Mrs. Kernstein, who had moved over from her home in Golders Green to look after Gita, filled her life with helping her seven married children whenever they needed her. By the time Mrs. Langfeld had arrived on Friday, she had prepared the *Shalom Zachor* and had cooked all the *Shabbos* meals.

Shabbos was quite relaxing and Mrs. Langfeld rested for the first time since the Pesach holidays. One of the things she enjoyed immensely was going to visit Nechy's mother. Although still a bit frail-looking, Mrs. Horowitz was a changed person, her bearing far more positive and her appearance much improved. Although still unable to afford a *sheitel*, she wore more brightly-colored headscarves, usually done up in a dignified turban style, and her clothes were simple, yet tasteful. She was working now and seemed to enjoy her job as a cook in a boys' *cheder*. Now she had a piece of good news to tell Mrs. Langfeld. She had found a flat at last! It was a pleasant, self-contained two-bedroom flat quite near the Myersons' house. She told Mrs. Langfeld how much she was looking forward to moving into it the following weekend.

They talked about Nechy and then the conversation steered round to Shulamis.

"She's such a lovely girl!" Mrs. Horowitz declared. "I'm so satisfied Nechy has her for a friend. She's done so much for her."

"Yes, she is an exceptional girl," Mrs. Langfeld agreed.

"I hope she'll look upon our flat as her home," Mrs. Horowitz went on. "Poor thing, she's got no one. I'd like to be like a mother to her…" There was a thoughtful expression on her face and she looked as if she was about to say something. Then she seemed to change her mind and went on to discuss practical things, asking the headmistress if she would allow Nechy time off from school so that Nechy could help her move, to which Mrs. Langfeld readily agreed.

Once the *bris* was over and, after helping to clear up from the *seudah*, Mrs. Langfeld spent her last afternoon helping Gita to pacify little Aryeh, who was perfectly adorable, even when he cried!

In the evening, her friend Dina Weiss came round to visit her. It was then she remembered the problem she had been shelving.

Dina was shocked when she heard her proposal. It had been due to Dina's help that Mrs. Langfeld had been able to purchase Kettering Manor, as the house had been called. She had bustled about enthusiastically, collecting financial support until enough money had been raised. Now it practically broke her heart to think of her friend being forced to move away from it!

"I can't understand you, Minna!" she protested. "You've always been one to rise to a challenge! How can you let one individual with a bee in his bonnet drive you out! You know yourself how much that house means to you…and it seemed so *bashert* the way it fell into your hands like that! I think you should stick to to your guns and not let this chap get the better of you!" Her tone was emphatic, making it difficult for Mrs. Langfeld to argue.

Nochum Tzvi, however, was more understanding of his mother's point of view. As they sat talking later that night, he gave the matter a great deal of thought.

"You're right really," he said. "I can understand how you feel about the place, but don't forget I've met the fellow and he strikes me as dangerous. He could cause you no end of trouble, so, if you find another place—which won't be easy—I would grab it, if I were you!"

Travelling back to school the next morning, Mrs. Langfeld could no longer conjure up the feeling of relaxation she had enjoyed over Shabbos. The old state of tension had returned as she reflected on the dilemma that faced her.

To whom should she listen? Dina or Nochum Tzvi? Dina's wonderful enthusiasm was refreshing, she knew, but she was an idealist, after all. Nochum Tzvi was more realistic and practical, and she realized with a sinking heart, that his argument was what she had felt all along as well!

A HOME AT LAST

"**S**HULAMIS, CAN I SHOW YOU SOMETHING?" Coming out of the art room, Nechy called across the hall to her friend, who was on her way to the common room. As Nechy approached her , Shulamis noticed a large, flat object tucked mysteriously under the other girl's arm. Without waiting for a reply, Nechy took it out and held it toward Shulamis for her inspection.

Shulamis, realizing at once that it was a painting, took the canvas board in her hands and looked down at it. Painted in soft, subtle shades, it depicted a forest scene in winter, the bare trees erect and dignified, with their gnarled, leafless branches thrust outward. Brown, gravelly paths wound through dark-leafed evergreen bushes and here and there some squirrels and birds, including a robin, could be seen.

"Did you paint this?" she asked Nechy.

"Yes. Don't you recognize it?"

Shulamis peered at the painting once more. There was something familiar about it but she couldn't quite place it.

She seemed to remember being in a forest just like that. Then, like a flash, it came to her.

"Epping Forest!" she exclaimed triumphantly.

"That's right. Do you like it?" Nechy asked shyly.

"Like it?" Shulamis cried. "It's fabulous! Really gorgeous! When did you paint it?"

"I did a bit of sketching in the forest when I went down to Chingford, the first time after you'd been there with me!" Nechy told her. "Miss Feinbaum taught me how to draw it onto the canvas and paint it. It's going to be a present for Mummy, for the new flat."

"Oh she'll love it!" Shulamis said enthusiastically. "Are you going to have it framed?"

"Yes. Miss Feinbaum's cousin has a picture framing shop in London. She told me she would write and ask him to do it very cheaply for me—I'd never be able to afford it otherwise! You know Mummy's moving on Sunday, don't you? Well, I'm going down to help her. Mrs. Langfeld said I could."

"I should think so! It stands to reason," Shulamis began.

"Shulamis?" Nechy cut it, her expression tentative, "do you think she would let you come too?"

"What, me?" Shulamis said, surprise and embarrassment in her voice. "You don't want me there!"

"Of course I do!" Nechy declared, "I wouldn't ask you if I didn't!"

"But what about your mother? She might not like it. I'll feel like an intruder!"

"Don't be silly! You're nothing of the sort! I know Mummy would love you to come. When I suggested it to her she said she'd thought of it too, but didn't like to ask Mrs. Langfeld."

"But why would you need me?" Shulamis still sounded baffled. "Surely you'd rather be on your own with your mother while she's setting up house. I'd just be in the way!"

"Well, actually I could do with your touch," Nechy said persuasively. "You're much better than me at arranging things to look nice. Do you remember when we shared a room how nice you made it?"

"Hey! You're the artistic one, not me!"

"But that's different," Nechy argued. "I'm not methodical, like you."

"Well, if you put it like that," Shulamis laughed. "How can I say no? Let's see what Mrs. Langfeld says. She might not be happy about it, since it's so near to exams."

Mrs. Langfeld did consent, however, provided Shulamis did not fall behind with her studying.

Sunday morning, therefore, found the girls on the early train to London. They were met at the station by Mr. Myerson, who drove them to his house, assuring Nechy that her mother had already completed her packing and was all ready for the move.

As they rode along Stamford Hill, Nechy peered out of the window, looking out for the picture framing shop belonging to Miss Feinbaum's cousin. Suddenly she spotted it.

"There it is!" she cried triumphantly. "RUBIN'S FRAMING CO. Mr. Myerson, do you mind if we stop here for a moment? It won't take long."

"Sure!" Nodding patiently, Mr. Myerson pulled up outside the shop and the two girls got out and hurried inside.

Mr. Rubin, a benevolent-looking gentleman with a ginger beard and thick, dark-rimmed spectacles, scanned the note, Miss Feinbaum, the art teacher, had written and beamed at the girls.

"Ah, yes! How is my cousin? My wife was just saying the other day that we haven't heard from her for a while." He picked up Nechy's painting and examined it. "Very nice," he commented, "anywhere special, is it?"

"Yes, it's Epping Forest," Nechy explained.

"Ah yes, Epping Forest. My son went there on *Lag B'omer*." he perused the letter again, then peered at Nechy for a moment. "So you're Mrs. Horowitz's daughter, are you? Well, I'll tell you what. My cousin asked me to make a special price for you, but, because your mother is the new cook at the *cheder* my little Yoini goes to, I'll do it for you for nothing!"

"Oh no." Nechy began, embarrassed. "I didn't want—"

But Mr. Rubin held up his hand to wave away her protests. "I insist!" he said emphatically. "So *don't* argue! It'll be ready on Tuesday afternoon."

"Oh." Nechy's face fell. How could she have the cheek to ask him to do it quickly when he wasn't even charging her for it? "Er...you see...we're only here till tomorrow afternoon. We've got to go back to school..."

"O.K., O.K.!" Mr. Rubin's tone was placating. "I'll do a rush job and have it finished for lunchtime tomorrow, then."

"Oh, thank you so much!" Nechy brightened up immediately. "It's very kind of you!"

"Well I can't have my cousin saying I didn't treat you well!" Mr. Rubin laughed jovially, sticking half a ticket onto the painting and handing Nechy the other half. "After twelve tomorrow then. O.K.?"

Nechy thanked him profusely once more and, with Shulamis behind her, she hurried out of the shop, her eyes sparkling with excitement.

The girls liked the flat as soon as they saw it, even in its bare state. Sunlight streamed into the little square hall, from where they could see into all the rooms the doors having been left open. The dining room, which also served as the living room, to their left, looked spacious and welcoming, freshly decorated with a charming wallpaper. Next to it was a fairly small, but well-equipped kitchen with a little, formica-topped table against one wall, surrounded by four steel chairs. There were two medium-sized bedrooms on either side of a green and white-tiled bathroom.

Nechy stole a glance at her mother, wondering if she, too, liked the flat. It was hard to interpret Mrs Horowitz's expression, although it was obvious that some strong emotion was passing through the woman's mind.

In fact, it was a variety of feelings that Mrs. Horowitz was experiencing. Her first reaction, having already seen the flat once, was that it looked inviting. Then the realization hit her that this was now her home and, without warning, a picture sprang up in front of her eyes. She saw a small brick house with a wooden green door, flanked on either side, by prettily-curtained bay windows. On the left-hand side of the house, a little further back, an old apple tree stood. It was the house in Czechoslovakia, where she had lived straight after her marriage. For a fleeting moment, she saw a baby carriage in front of the house with a baby boy sitting in it and a blonde, curly-haired little girl standing next to it. Hastily, she shut the memory out. She would break down in tears if she allowed her mind to dwell on her two older children, Perele and Hershy.

At that point, mercifully, the scene changed and she could see the pleasant pale-green kitchen of their flat in Antwerp, where a ginger-haired baby girl of a few months was sitting in a high chair. Nechy! Her little Nechy! Involuntarily, her gaze flew to her daughter, standing beside her and eyeing her anxiously. Bracing herself, she pulled herself back to the present. *Boruch Hashem* she still had Nechy...and if this was to be her home from now on, she had better make the best of it—if not for her own sake, then for Nechy's sake!

Most of the furniture, which Mrs. Horowitz had bought partly with some of her wages and partly with money she had received from a *Gemillas Chesed* fund—specially set up to help war refugees—was still standing in the hall, having been delivered on Friday. Only the large pieces, such as cupboards and beds, had been put in place by the delivery men. Nechy and Shulamis set to work immediately, moving the rest about, amid much discussion and re-arranging, until it was all placed to everyone's satisfaction.

Mrs. Horowitz had received quite a few gifts and lots of donations which the girls enjoyed putting around the flat. There was an attractive mirrored hall stand from the Myersons and a tapestry of *Kever Rochel*, hand-embroidered by one of the neighbors, as well as a charming *Mizrach* that had been painted by one of the Myersons' grandchildren. Mrs. Langfeld had instructed Nochum Tzvi to buy something and he had brought round a crystal vase, which Shulamis placed on the dining room table, making a mental note to buy some flowers for it the next morning.

Nechy ear-marked a spot on the wall of the dining room for the painting, whispering her intention to Shulamis when her mother out of earshot.

By the time all the curtains were hung up and the essentials put in place it was quite late and Mrs. Horowitz went into the kitchen to heat up the meal Mrs. Myerson had sent round, insisting they stop working for the night.

"We can finish the unpacking tomorrow morning," she said. "I don't have to go to work tomorrow as I've been given the day off."

They sat round the little kitchen table cozily, eating supper. Then Nechy suddenly remembered the parcel from Dr.

Sykora.

Late that afternoon, the doctor had knocked at the door but had refused Nechy's invitation to come in.

"No, I can see you're very busy…and I'm on my way to see a patient. I'll come when your mother is settled, but I wanted to give her this. I'm sure she'll like it because it's something that was quite popular in Czechoslovakia before the war. A relative of mine, who lives in Devon, still does this kind of embroidery and sells it, so I bought one for your mother. Please give her my regards and wish her much happiness here. I'll come to see her some time next week."

Nechy had taken the parcel inside intending to give it to her mother when she and Shulamis had finished hanging the bedroom curtains, but she had ended up forgetting all about it. Now she produced it and Mrs. Horowitz tore open the pretty, red wrapping and pulled out a tablecloth. Made of cream linen, it was exquisitely embroidered with an array of poppies and bright yellow sunflowers. Each bloom was gradually shaded and seemed to stand out, giving it a three-dimensional effect.

"It's gorgeous!" Nechy exclaimed, drawing a deep breath and letting it out slowly.

"It's absolutely stunning!" Shulamis declared.

The girls looked toward Mrs. Horowitz, waiting for her comment, but, to their shock and horror, they saw that she had turned deathly pale and was no longer looking at the tablecloth. The old Mrs. Horowitz, it seemed, was back. Haunted and drawn, she reached for the tablecloth and threw it on the floor.

"Take it away!" she whispered hoarsely. "I can't look at it!"

"B-but Mummy…" Nechy stammered, puzzled and anxious, "What's wrong?"

"It reminds me…" Mrs. Horowitz began, her voice choked.

But the sight of her daughter's worried face made her compose herself slightly and she carried on in a more controlled tone. "I used to have a tablecloth just like this. It was really very similar. My mother embroidered it for me before my *chasunah*." Her voice began to falter again, "She embroidered so beautifully...just like that...*Oy, Mamme! Mamme!*..." She sat down at the table and covered her face with her hands, sobbing bitterly. Not knowing what to do or say, Nechy stood with her arm across her mother's shoulders, waiting patiently for her mother's weeping to cease, while she and Shulamis eyed each other with concern.

Presently, Mrs. Horowitz pulled herself together once more and, wiping her eyes, gave the girls a ghost of a smile.

"What's the use of crying," she said with a deep sigh, "it won't bring her back—and it won't undo what happened." She stood up and began to collect the dishes, taking them to the sink. Nechy picked up the tablecloth and, replacing it in the wrapping paper, took it into the dining room and threw it into a corner. No more was said about the incident, but the previous cozy atmosphere was gone.

The screams that woke the two girls around three in the morning did not come as a complete surprise. Nechy slipped out of bed and hurried to her mother's room, where she remained for a very long time—or so it seemed to Shulamis.

"She's sleeping now," Nechy told her friend. "I gave her one of the stronger sedatives. I'm so stupid! I should have given her something before she went to bed!"

"Well, how were you to know?" Shulamis tried to console her.

"I thought she'd got over everything," Nechy said sadly, "but she obviously hasn't. This seems to have knocked her right back again!"

The next morning, however, Mrs. Horowitz seemed perfectly in control—almost as if nothing had happened. Shulamis, feeling she ought to leave mother and daughter alone together for a while, announced that she was slipping out to do some shopping, while Nechy and Mrs. Horowitz finished unpacking all the boxes of housewares and linens that had been donated. When Shulamis returned an hour later with the bunch of flowers, Mrs. Horowitz kissed her warmly, expressing her delight.

Later, Nechy went out to pick up her painting, giving her mother some vague excuse. Alone with Shulamis, Mrs. Horowitz took the opportunity to thank her for all she had done for Nechy.

"If not for you, Nechy would still be miserable and unhappy," she stated simply.

"Oh, but she's not like that really!" Shulamis began. Somehow, she found it quite easy to speak to Mrs. Horowitz, in spite of the language difficulty. She, too, had learned a bit of Yiddish and, by mixing that together with her rather inferior German, she managed to make herself understood.

"I know…" Mrs. Horowitz agreed. "She was such a good-natured child when she was little, always singing and laughing. It was seeing me so ill and weak that changed her and made her so serious. I put too heavy a burden on her!"

Shulamis opened her mouth to protest but Mrs. Horowitz went on. "Luckily, she has had you! You have been better than a sister to her!"

"We've always been like sisters," Shulamis murmured.

"I know…and I wish you really were sisters. Nechy needs a sister…to replace the one she had." There was a sad note in her voice, yet she found herself suddenly able to speak about Perele without breaking down. She eyed Shulamis searchingly and the girl did not know what to make of the expression. Feeling embarrassed, she quickly pulled one of the tea-chests containing dishes into the kitchen and began to unpack it, stopping for a moment to admire the attractive crockery before handing the pieces to Mrs. Horowitz to put away in the cupboards.

How kind people are, she thought, her eyes straying to the other boxes in the hall, all containing housewares and linens donated by members of the London community. She marvelled at the way Jews managed to help each other out in times of crisis.

Nechy, meanwhile, was making her way toward Mr. Rubin's shop when, on an impulse, she went into a telephone kiosk and dialed Dr. Sykora's number.

"Nechy? Is anything wrong?" the doctor sounded concerned.

"Oh, Dr. Sykora! I feel so bad to tell you this! That tablecloth you brought Mummy...well, it's absolutely stunning! But..." Before she could stop herself, she poured the whole story out to the doctor.

"I see." There was a moment's silence, making Nechy feel even worse. Then Dr. Sykora said, "Nechy, I'm terribly sorry! The last thing I would have wanted was to cause your mother to have a setback!"

"I only told you because I want to know what to do," Nechy said apologetically. "I thought you ought to know."

"Yes, you were quite right. But don't get down-hearted. The fact that she is back in control is a good sign, isn't it? She rebounded quickly and that is excellent."

"Yes, but what shall I do with the tablecloth?" Nechy was glad the doctor could not see her blushing with embarrassment. "Should I send it back to you? I mean...it's a shame to waste such a beautiful thing."

"No, don't do that. Put it away somewhere, underneath a pile of other things. Maybe, one day, your mother may take it out, glad that she has something that reminds her of your grandmother. And when she does that, you'll know she's well on the way to a complete recovery!"

Mrs. Horowitz and Shulamis were working in the kitchen when Nechy let herself quietly into the flat. They didn't notice her and she slipped into the dining room and unwrapped her picture. Mr. Rubin had certainly done it justice with the rustic brown frame, a thin line of gold at the inside edge setting the painting off well. Thankful that the clattering of dishes in the kitchen was so loud, she gently knocked a picture hook into the wall. Then she hung up the picture and stepped back to admire it. Epping Forest suddenly came to life as she looked at it and she was seized by a moment of panic. What if it had the same effect as the tablecloth? It might remind her mother of the nursing home, where she had been so terribly ill, and she might be thrown into despair once more. What had she done? Why hadn't she thought of it?

But it was too late to do anything about it.

"Nechy? Is that you?" Mrs. Horowitz had heard her and was coming in, followed by Shulamis.

"Yes, Mummy," Nechy said, collecting herself and hoping for the best. "Come and have a look at this!"

Mrs. Horowitz came and stood in front of the picture, recognizing the scene immediately.

"It's that forest near the nursing home," she announced. "Where did you find it?"

"I painted it," Nechy told her simply.

"What? All by yourself?" Mrs. Horowitz stared at her for a moment, the depth of expression in her blue-green eyes was so like Nechy's. Then she turned back to examine the picture and looked at Nechy once more.

Nechy nodded shyly and her mother threw her arms around her, hugging her tightly. "Nechy! My Nechele," she cried, her voice tearful, "I'm so proud of you!"

She released Nechy and held her at arms length for a moment. Then her gaze swept briefly round the lightly furnished room and rested on the painting again.

"I've been given so many lovely presents," she said, "but this is the one I shall treasure most of all!"

RECOGNITION

I T WAS A WEARY, DEPRESSED MRS. LANGFELD who let herself into the school building while everyone was in the dining room for supper. Hoping no one would come up and speak to her, she slipped quietly into her office and sat down at the desk. Picking up a pencil and drawing a notebook up in front of her, she jotted down a few figures, trying to take stock of the situation.

The building she had just been to view was the only one of all the places she had looked over that had possibilities. It was quite spacious and would accommodate the school comfortably. But she just did not feel drawn to it. It lacked the charm and warmth of "Beis Aryeh," as she had renamed Kettering Manor.

Stop it! she told herself. You must not compare every building to this one! Obviously, you feel sentimental and nostalgic toward it.

Yet, try as she might, she just could not picture Migdal Binoh in the house she had just seen. However, the move was a necessity and it seemed unlikely that she would find anything better. She would have to take the plunge and make an offer for the place.

Set in extensive grounds, the building, which was situated in a village in the neighboring county of Bedfordshire, had once belonged to a Peer and, although it had been empty for quite a while, it had been kept in a fairly good state of repair. The village itself was not as picturesque as Elmsleigh, having a more industrial atmosphere, as it accommodated a number of factories. But there was one advantage as far as Mrs. Langfeld was concerned. The house was not actually on a street or lane, being flanked on one side by a power station, and on the other by a wide, open field, and therefore there were no neighbors. That meant there was no chance of any more Mr. Campbells! Mrs. Langfeld felt a stab of anger as she thought of Mr. Campbell. It was entirely his fault that she was being forced to make this move!

She glanced at the figures she had written down and considered the options. The move would involve a fair amount of money as it would have to be adapted to their requirements and a lot depended on how much the sale of the present house brought in. Strangely enough, she had recently received a letter from an organization she had never heard of, offering her a good price, should she consider selling it. She could not help wondering whether Mr. Campbell was somehow involved and thus she regarded the offer with suspicion and mistrust.

The one person she felt obliged to speak to was Sir Isaac Greenhorn, the kind benefactor who had put up the money to buy Kettering Manor. It was only right that she should inform him of her intention. Sir Isaac tried to dissuade her at first, not happy for the school to move so far from his home in Chesham, but he understood her reasons and promised his financial support wherever necessary. Now that she had found a place worth considering, she resolved to go and see him again the next day.

But she would certainly not tell anyone else at school until things were quite settled, and definitely not before the school's Open Day, which was to take place the following week. It had been decided to hold the occasion out of doors, in the school grounds, and now that exams were over, teachers and pupils were busy preparing for it. The knowledge that they might not be in the same place next term could well dampen their enthusiasm.

It was not easy to keep the knowledge to herself, as she carried on with her negotiations. Once or twice, she toyed with the idea of confiding in her senior teacher, Mrs. Gold, but she resisted the urge.

She was all the more dismayed, therefore, when Mrs. Gold herself burst into the office a few days later, obviously immensely distressed. Her eyes looked heavy and there were signs that she had been in tears. What surprised Mrs. Langfeld most of all was the fact that she had rushed in without knocking.

"Minna!" she burst out immediately, "I just can't believe it! Tell me it isn't true!"

"Leah! What's the matter? Why are you so upset?"

"Of course I'm upset!" Mrs. Gold's voice rose an octave. "I heard last night that you're thinking of moving the school to another neighborhood! Is it true? I haven't slept all night, worrying about it!"

Mrs. Langfeld's heart sank. She didn't even have to ask how Mrs. Gold had obtained the information. It was quite obvious. Why hadn't she thought of telling Sir Isaac to keep it to himself? He must have assumed that all the teachers at the school knew about it.

"Yes, it is true," she said quietly.

"But why? And why didn't you tell me? You could have knocked me down with a feather when my husband told me last night. And he, of course, had to pretend he knew all about it when Sir Isaac mentioned it to him!"

"Oh Leah, I'm really sorry! I was sorely tempted to confide in you but I didn't think it was fair when you and the rest of the staff were so busy marking exam papers and now preparing for Open Day."

She had a sinking feeling when she thought of the forthcoming Open Day. This was a day when parents came to the school to take a good look at the premises and talk to the teachers and view their daughters' work. It was a day that was usually approached with pride and an atmosphere of festivity. But now...what was the use of displaying a place they would soon be vacating? If only they could put it off! But it was too late for that. Arrangements were already in progress.

"But why would you want to move?" Mrs. Gold demanded, sounding perplexed. "What's wrong with this place?"

Mrs. Langfeld sighed. "Believe me, Leah, it's the last thing I really want." She went on to explain her reasons and Mrs. Gold listened with a solemn expression.

"Yes, I do understand," she said, soberly, "but I still wish you would change your mind. I shall be sorry to leave."

"Leave?" Mrs. Langfeld stared at her, aghast. "But why?"

"How do you think I'll be able to get from Chesham to Bedfordshire every morning? You've forgotten, I don't live in, like the others."

Mrs. Langfeld experienced the sinking feeling once more. She really had forgotten. And Mrs. Gold, who was, in a sense, her right hand, was the one teacher she felt she could not dispense with. Close to her own age, Leah Gold, with her broad shoulders and square, resolute chin, was a rock to be relied on, and provided Mrs. Langfeld with a sense of companionship.

"Oh Leah!" she cried. "It's true. I hadn't thought! And I really need you here! What shall I do?"

"Why couldn't you find somewhere nearer?" Mrs. Gold wanted to know.

"Because I wanted to get away from Buckinghamshire altogether. Now that Mr. Campbell has become involved in local affairs his influence can be quite far-reaching. But I will have to abandon the whole idea! I can't sacrifice you for it."

"No," Mrs. Gold protested. "I don't want to be responsible for putting the school or the pupils in jeopardy! You'll have to carry on with it. Don't worry. Even if I leave, I'll still keep in touch."

"Well, maybe we can still find a solution," Mrs. Langfeld said, trying to sound hopeful.

"Maybe…," Mrs. Gold echoed, though her tone was skeptical.

Tuesday began with a hazy mist and a general murmur of disappointment rippled through the school as the girls expressed their fears that Open Day would have to be held indoors after all.

"There goes our Garden Party," Etty remarked to Mrs. Langfeld and was treated to a non-committal grunt in reply. Etty eyed her narrowly, wondering why the idea should upset her mother so much. "Cheer up, Mummy," she said. "It won't be all that bad if we have to stay inside!"

The comment gave Mrs. Langfeld a jolt. Etty may have misinterpreted the reason for her despondency but it made her realize that her facade had slipped. Until now Mrs. Langfeld had managed to hide her feelings but, unable to rid her mind of the fact that tomorrow was the day arranged for her to put down a deposit on the property in Bedfordshire, she occasionally forgot to hide her feelings. Making an effort to smile brightly, she patted her daughter and said, "It's only half-past-eight! The weather could easily brighten up by the afternoon!"

As it turned out, she was proved right. By mid-morning the sun had burst through, bright and warm and there was a frantic rush to transfer the tables and equipment outside and give the grounds a festive look.

Everyone was busy. Stalls were set up, displaying work done by the girls, such as arts and crafts and needlework of different kinds. In addition, one stall displayed an assortment of cakes and dishes produced by the pupils who excelled in cooking lessons.

Supervising the preparations, Mrs. Langfeld circulated around with an encouraging smile for everyone. Yet she could not help a feeling of sadness, seeing how pleasant and welcoming the grounds looked. The lawns had been freshly mown and the bushes surrounding the lawn were neatly trimmed. Even the concrete playground area looked festive, with stalls set out colorfully all around. It's really a sort of farewell party to the house, she reflected, though nobody knows it!

Banners, attractively painted with messages such as "BERUCHIM HABAIM" and "WELCOME TO MIGDAL BINOH," were hung on trees by Miss Feinbaum, the art teacher, with the help of Nechy, Judy Kleiner and a few other artistic girls, who had been responsible for painting them.

"Lovely!" the headmistress commented. "They're absolutely beautifully done!" Then, addressing Nechy, she said, "I believe your mother is coming to Open Day. How nice for you! This is the first year you are having her visit you at school!"

"I know. It's incredible isn't it?" Nechy's voice portrayed her excitement. Her eyes, wet and beginning to tear, were Mrs. Langfeld's reminder of what a miracle it was that she had her mother back.

"How is she getting here?" Mrs. Langfeld asked.

"Yitty Lieber's parents are bringing her with them in the car," Nechy told her. "She's really looking forward to it! She's glad she's going to see the place where I'll be spending the best part of the next two years. She says I won't seem so far away if she can picture my surroundings."

Mrs. Langfeld nodded, though Nechy's words gave her a pang and also made her feel guilty. This secret had consequences she hadn't thought of. Now Mrs. Horowitz was coming here under a misapprehension, imagining she was seeing the place where Nechy would spend the next two years.

Giving an almost inaudible sigh, she moved on to oversee the installation of the loudspeaker system, resolving to push her worries to the back of her mind and do her best to give the occasion a cheerful and festive atmosphere!

"I would like to welcome you all to our school for our first Open Day," Mrs. Langfeld's voice resounded through the loudspeakers that had been strategically placed around the grounds. "I am not going to make a speech—we hold a Speech Day in the winter for that purpose." Laughter rippled through the large crowd of parents and pupils. "The object of today's occasion is to let you view your daughters' achievements. As you can see, samples of their work are displayed on stalls around the grounds. You can also discuss their progress with the teachers, who are circulating about, each one wearing a badge with her name printed on it. Refreshments are being served continually in the blue and white striped marquee near the entrance, and I can tell you that everything there is quite delicious, thanks to our exceptional cook, Mrs. Hoffman!" The girls all cheered and applauded loudly at this. "That is all I have to say for now," Mrs. Langfeld went on, "except to wish you all a very pleasant afternoon!"

Another round of applause greeted the end of her speech, after which soft background music was transmitted through the loudspeakers from inside the house, as pupils, parents and teachers began to mingle and converse.

Standing near Mrs. Gold, who, like the headmistress, had resolved to shelve her own feeling of desolation for the afternoon, Mrs. Langfeld saw Mrs. Horowitz coming toward her.

"Mrs. Horowitz!" she cried cordially, shaking her hand, "how nice to see you! I'm so glad you could come! Have you settled well in your flat?"

"Yes, thank you, Mrs. Langfeld," Mrs Horowitz replied, able to understand Mrs. Langfeld's German but answering in Yiddish, nevertheless. "I've been looking forward to coming here since Nechy told me about it. It's good to see the place that has been my daughter's home for so long!"

"Well, I'm glad she's got a real home now!" Mrs. Langfeld said. "Let me introduce you to Mrs. Gold, who teaches history and English. Leah, this is Nechy's mother, as you must have gathered."

The two women shook hands and Mrs. Gold began talking in fluent Yiddish, much to Mrs. Horowitz's delight.

Leaving them to it, Mrs. Langfeld turned round to see if anyone else wished to speak to her when, to her horror, she saw, striding purposefully toward her, the stocky figure of Mr. Campbell, clad in a beige checked shirt and brown corduroy trousers.

What does he want this time? she thought, noticing the grim expression on his face.

"Mrs. Langfeld, do you have to have all this noise going on?" he demanded, when he reached her. "My wife has one of her migraine headaches and it's disturbing her."

"I'm sorry, Mr. Campbell," Mrs. Langfeld replied, as politely as she could, suppressing her irritation, "but I don't think you can call this 'noise.' The music is not loud at all and you can't expect people not to talk. It is an Open Day, after all!"

"But why must you hold it out of doors? I would appreciate it if you would move everything back into the house."

Mrs. Langfeld's patience snapped. There was no end to this man's troublemaking! Why couldn't he leave them in peace? Until now, she had tried her best to be civil and not antagonize him, but since they would not be neighbors for long, she decided to stand up to him.

"No!" she said decisively, "I will do nothing of the sort! There is no reason why we should not hold an outdoor activity in the middle of the day. If your wife is prone to migraine attacks you should not have bought a house so near to a school! Now, if you don't mind, would you please leave the school grounds and not disturb me. I have a lot of parents to speak to."

Mr. Campbell's face darkened with rage. "How dare you, you stupid cow!" he thundered.

Mrs. Langfeld was shocked by his words and hoped that none of the girls had heard him. She opened her mouth to request him to mind his language in front of her pupils, but was stopped by an agonized shriek behind her.

"*Nein! Nein!*" the voice cried, "*WOLTER!!*"

Mrs. Langfeld turned round to see Mrs. Horowitz staring

at Mr. Campbell, an expression of recognition on her chalk white face. Seeing her begin to sway, Mrs. Langfeld and Mrs. Gold instinctively put out their arms and just managed to catch her as she fainted.

SHOWDOWN

"**W**HAT HAPPENED?" Mrs. Langfeld asked, as she and Mrs. Gold bent over the prostrate figure of Mrs. Horowitz, whom they had placed gently on the ground, a rolled up rug supporting her head. The poor woman's breathing was short and shallow and she gave an occasional moan, but she had not yet regained full consciousness. The headmistress had sent one of the girls to fetch a glass of water and another to find Miss Zemmel. Until they returned, there was nothing they could do but watch over her.

"I don't really know," Mrs. Gold said, in reply to Mrs. Langfeld's question, "I was talking to her while you were arguing with Mr. Campbell."

Mr. Campbell! In the panic Mrs. Langfeld had forgotten all about him! She looked up toward the spot where she had been talking to him, wondering how he was reacting to all this, but there was no sign of him.

"...and when he raised his voice," Mrs. Gold was saying,

"her eyes suddenly opened wide and she really looked as if she had seen a ghost. Her face went as white as a sheet even before she turned round and when she did she let out that terrible shriek. And…well…you know the rest."

Mrs. Langfeld nodded, looking puzzled. Whatever could it all mean?

The girl who had been sent for the water returned, with Miss Zemmel hard on her heels. By now people had begun to realize that something unusual had occurred and a crowd began to gather around Mrs. Horowitz.

"Mummy! Mummy! What's happened?" With an anguished cry, Nechy pushed her way through the crowd and dropped down beside her mother.

"She fainted," Mrs. Langfeld told her gently, trying to sound reassuring, "it could be the heat."

Miss Zemmel, meanwhile, was holding water to the unconscious woman's lips and slowly Mrs. Horowitz's color returned and she opened her eyes. For a few moments she looked round, her expression blank, then awareness came to her and the color began to drain away again. She began to speak in Yiddish, her tone agitated.

"*Wuss tit ehr du?* What is he doing here?" she cried, "that beast Wollter! Why has he followed me here? Hasn't he done enough to me? And enough to my mother? He's a murderer! He killed my mother, the *roshah!*"

A strangled cry escaped from Nechy. She grabbed her mother's hand and clasped it tightly. Mrs. Langfeld and Mrs. Gold exchanged glances, realization passing between them. Mrs. Langfeld felt an immense feeling of relief. She now knew that Mr. Campbell was not just the run of the mill annoying neighbor! So that was why Mr. Campbell had disappeared so suddenly! Something had to be done immediately, the headmistress knew, or he would slip through the net! But there was Mrs. Horowitz to see to.

"Miss Zemmel," she said, "I think you and Mrs. Gold should take Mrs. Horowitz inside and look after her. I have to make an urgent phone call!"

Leaving them to follow her instructions, she ran into the office and put through a call to Superintendent Blake.

The Superintendent listened with interest and surprise. "So," he said at last, "you were on the right track after all! I owe you an apology. But we must act promptly if we want to catch him. I shall come down at once, with a couple of my men. If you wish, you can meet us outside his cottage in five minutes. I hope we're not too late!"

"I'll be there," Mrs. Langfeld promised and hung up.

She looked into the reception room, where Mrs. Horowitz had been taken, and saw that she was sitting in an armchair, talking to Mrs. Gold, Miss Zemmel and Nechy, who were all listening intently to her words. Breathing a sigh of relief, Mrs. Langfeld called out that she would be back soon and hurried out of the house.

Getting out of the grounds was no easy task. Parents, as well as some of the teachers, kept waylaying her, mostly to ask how Mrs. Horowitz was, but she managed to disentangle herself and she hurried down the lane to "The Willows," Mr. Campbell's cottage, as fast as she could.

She arrived there to find Superintendent Blake talking to the driver of a cab that had just driven up.

"'Ere! What's goin' on?" the driver was obviously annoyed. "Why should I go away? I'm supposed to pick up a fare 'ere."

"Well your services will not be required after all," the Superintendent told him.

"Yeah? 'OO says so? I'm not goin' nowhere till I've been paid the minimum fare, at least!" the driver protested.

Blake took out his identification card and showed it to

him. The driver's eyes opened wide.

"Police, eh?" he exclaimed. "Well, I ain't getting mixed up in no funny business! So long, guv!" and he sped off down the lane.

"At least we know the bird hasn't flown yet," Superintendent Blake remarked to Mrs. Langfeld. "I see the front door's open and there are some suitcases on the porch. They're obviously waiting for that cab. Perhaps we can sneak inside and pick up a bit of incriminating evidence."

"Isn't the fact that they're trying to abscond incriminating enough?" Mrs. Langfeld suggested.

"Perhaps. I'm not sure how much weight that would carry in court though." Instructing two policemen who were standing around to follow in a few moments and wait round the side of the house, the Superintendent began to creep surreptitiously up the path. Feeling slightly ridiculous, Mrs. Langfeld followed suit.

Sneaking into the house, they hid behind the open door and listened. A heated argument was in progress.

"Emily!" Mr. Campbell was shouting, "leave that stupid rug and come! We've got to hurry!"

"But it's a valuable rug!" Mrs. Campbell's plaintive voice could be heard. "Great Aunt Jane left it to me..."

"You don't seem to understand!" Mr. Campbell sounded irritated. "We've got to get away quickly! *I HAVE BEEN REC-OGNIZED!!*"

"It serves you right!" Mrs. Campbell cried shrilly, "I warned you, didn't I? As soon as we found out that school was a Jewish school I was afraid this might happen. I begged you to move away but—oh no! You had to be the clever one! 'Leave it to me!' you said," she mimicked her husband's tone, "'I'll make that headmistress move her school away, see if I don't. Well, you did nothing of the sort! The school is still there…and now someone *has* recognized you!"

"All right! Don't gloat!" Mr. Campbell hissed, through clenched teeth. He was coming out into the hall as he spoke. "I don't know how that woman managed to survive," he mumbled grumpily, "she was more dead than alive when they were liberated. Where's that taxi? It should be…OOPS!" he looked up in surprise as he walked straight into Superintendent Blake, who had stepped out of his hiding place. "What in the world?! How dare you enter my house uninvited?"

"Mr. Campbell?" the police officer spoke sternly, "will you please step back into the room. We have some talking to do!"

"I beg your pardon?" Mr. Campbell looked indignant. "What is all this about? My wife and I are just about to leave for our holiday in Scotland. We have a taxi waiting."

"Correction!" Blake declared, "you *had* a taxi waiting. I sent your taxi away."

"You *what?!*" Mr. Campbell spluttered angrily.

He stared, dumbfounded, when the Superintendent produced his card and search warrant. Then he seemed to explode with fury.

"What is this? Are you arresting me? I have done nothing wrong! I'll have you know I'm a law abiding citizen."

"Law abiding according to Nazi standards maybe," Blake's tone was cold and sarcastic, "but this is England. Our job is to track down war criminals."

Mrs. Langfeld decided it was time she emerged from hiding too and, as soon as he saw her, Mr. Campbell gave a shout of triumph.

"Aha!" he yelled, pointing an accusing finger at her, "so *you're* behind this! I tell you, officer, she would stop at nothing to get me out of the way! Just because I am the only one with the courage to criticize the way she runs her school."

Mrs. Campbell had come out into the hall by then, but

Superintendent Blake pushed them both back into the living room, which was in a state of utter chaos, furniture and other articles having been thrown about frantically.

Mr. Campbell was still protesting loudly. "Who do you think you are…treating us like criminals? I'm not a war criminal! I was born in Scotland and I've been there all through the war."

"Kommandant Wollter! *Du bisst ehr!*" A voice rang out all of a sudden from the doorway. Everyone turned around at once, shocked to see Mrs. Horowitz standing there, Mrs. Gold, Miss Zemmel and Nechy behind her.

In spite of himself, Mr. Campbell blanched.

"*Nein!*" he cried involuntarily, in German, "*du lügst!* You are lying!"

There were gasps of surprise from all, except Mrs. Campbell, who exclaimed, in a harsh whisper, "Gerald! you fool!"

Her husband threw her a warning glance and tried to bluff it out. "What's so surprising? I learned German at school," he remarked airily. "I got an A in it, too!"

Mrs. Langfeld's mind suddenly flew back to the 'bomb incident.' Oh, so he was the one, she thought, as light dawned on her. He overheard my conversation in German with Miss Zemmel. However, that seemed in the distant past at the moment. She cast a look of concern at Mrs. Horowitz, wondering if she would withstand the ordeal of confronting the man who had caused her so much suffering and misery. Why had Mrs. Gold and Miss Zemmel brought her along? *She*, herself, would certainly not have allowed it.

Mrs. Horowitz, though pale and shaking visibly, was eyeing Mr. Campbell with a steady, unwavering gaze, making him flinch and look away.

"Yes, it is you!" she said coldly, speaking in a broken

German. "Your cruel face will be imprinted on my mind forever! And now I understand that the language you often spoke was English! You used an expression when you shouted at Mrs. Langfeld that you often used in the *lager*. As soon as I heard it I recognized your voice. Then I turned round and to my incredible surprise I saw your face." She closed her eyes for a moment and swayed a little. Miss Zemmel put her arm out but Mrs. Horowitz steadied herself and looked directly at Mr. Campbell again.

"*Der Leiber G-tt* will punish you for what you did to all of us!" she said, her voice piercing and accusing, "and specially for killing my mother! Don't think I will ever forget! You killed her with your own bare hands!"

"Rubbish!" Mr. Campbell snapped, "I don't know who you are—or what you're talking about, you stupid cow."

"There!" Mrs. Horowitz's voice held a note of triumph, although her German was still shaky and dotted with Yiddish, "that was it! That's exactly what you called my mother when you hit her! You said she was disobeying your orders! But it was because she wanted to obey the orders of her Maker! You tried to make her eat when she had to fast on *Yom Kippur*, and not only that, you wanted to force her to eat *treifa* meat. And when she refused, you beat her and beat her till she dropped down dead! And you did this all in front of *me*!"

Nechy, whom no one had realized was in the room, began to sob, putting her head on her mother's shoulder. Mrs. Horowitz put her arm round her and patted her comfortingly, suddenly in charge and facing her enemy.

Mr. Campbell appeared to be losing his composure, though he kept his lips pressed firmly together in a defiant manner. His wife, however, sensing that the game was up, had edged her way slowly to the door. Superintendent Blake, who was getting the translation of all that Mrs. Horowitz said from Mrs. Langfeld, suddenly noticed Mrs. Campbell and closed the door, barring her exit.

"Oh no you don't!" he said firmly. "You stay here and face the music with your husband!"

"Why should I?" she protested. "I never did anything! I might have lived in Germany, but I was not involved in any Nazi activity. In fact, I was quite friendly with a lot of the Jews."

"Oh yes?" her husband called out derisively. "What about the Klugmans, next door? You didn't have any scruples about giving them away to the Gestapo, did you?"

As soon as the words were out of his mouth he seemed to regret them. Biting his lip, he looked noticeably annoyed with himself. Mrs. Campbell, unable to reply, clenched her fists and glared at him angrily.

"I think we've heard enough now to arrest them," Blake announced, blowing a whistle to summon the two policemen who had been waiting outside. "I must admit I didn't understand everything, but there are enough of you who can testify to what was said. And we heard plenty in English that was incriminating. Gerald Campbell, alias…er…?" he looked at Mrs. Horowitz, who had no idea what he was after. It was Mrs. Langfeld who told him what he wanted to know. "Wollter," she said, glad she remembered.

Superintendent Blake finished cautioning Mr. and Mrs. Campbell—alias Wollter—and the couple were led away by the two policemen, with Mr. Campbell protesting loudly.

Mrs. Gold picked up one of the chairs that were lying on the floor and Mrs. Zemmel and Nechy sat Mrs. Horowitz down on it. She sat down gingerly, obviously finding it abhorrent to sit on one of *their* chairs, but she was grateful for the seat, nevertheless. She seemed utterly spent and exhausted. Mrs. Langfeld eyed her anxiously.

"Why did you bring her?" she asked, disapprovingly. "This has all been too much for her!"

"She insisted!" Mrs. Gold cried defensively. "As soon as she knew where you'd gone she declared that it was her duty to unmask the villain! We tried to stop her but we couldn't! She became really determined!"

"Well I, for one, am glad you didn't!" Blake remarked. "I didn't understand all of what this lady said but I'm sure that it was her arrival here and what she said that finally unnerved him. Am I right?"

Mrs. Langfeld nodded. "Yes, Officer, I think you are." She stole a glance at Mrs. Horowitz and saw that, although she still looked weak and pale, there was a certain new gleam in her eye. A gleam of satisfaction—and also of relief. She turned back to address the Superintendent. "It must have been a terrible ordeal for her," she said, "but I think you could say that she has laid down a ghost. Perhaps, now that she has, in a sense, finally avenged her mother's death, she will be able to come to terms with her dreadful experiences in the concentration camps and get over them at last!"

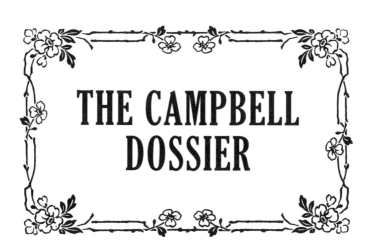

THE CAMPBELL DOSSIER

MR. CAMPBELL'S ARREST BECAME HEADLINE news nationwide, but nothing surpassed the interest—and, indeed, the surprise—of the inhabitants of Elmsleigh and the surrounding villages of Buckinghamshire. The villagers could not get over the fact that, just two days before the local Council elections, one of the candidates had been taken into custody by the police! Needless to say, there was no time to select a substitute, leaving the party he stood for under-represented.

Mr. Dobson telephoned Mrs. Langfeld the day after the arrest, expressing his utter astonishment.

"I'm absolutely flabbergasted!" he said. "I can't believe that we were hoodwinked by the fellow's charm. He took us all in!"

Not exactly *all*, Mrs. Langfeld thought to herself, but she refrained from making the comment.

Incredibly relieved that the heavy cloud hanging over the school had been finaly removed, Mrs. Langfeld went about the business of preparing for the end of term—and the school year—thinking she would hear no more of the affair until the trial. She was so absolutely thrilled that she would not have to move the school afterall and that all her troubles seemed finally over.

However, a week later, she received a telephone call from Superintendent Blake, informing her that Scotland Yard detectives had been quick and efficient in investigating Mr. Campbell's background and had prepared a dossier, a copy of which was on the way to her by special messenger.

She read the report with interest. It was indeed fascinating, and clarified a few things that had been puzzling her. How, for instance, did he come to be so fluently bilingual? And what was an Englishman—or rather, Scotsman—doing as a Nazi officer with a German name? This extensive file explained it all.

She decided to put a few people in the picture. Those who had witnessed the scene at "The Willows," namely Nechy, Mrs. Gold and Miss Zemmel, not to mention Mrs. Horowitz, all deserved to know the true story. Then there was Shulamis, who was so closely involved in anything to do with Nechy and her mother.

She arranged a time for the two girls, the teacher and the matron to congregate in her office. News of the meeting came to Etty's ears and she insisted on being invited too.

"Etty!" her mother protested, "this is not supposed to be common knowledge! I can't let everyone in on it. I might as well broadcast it to the whole school!"

"But Mummy!" Etty argued. "You can't say I'm not involved! After all, I did find that paint-tin and the brush, didn't I?"

She looked so earnest that Mrs. Langfeld had to laugh. "All right," she concurred, "but remember, it's *strictly* confidential. You are not to talk about it to *anyone!*"

The headmistress's office seemed rather overcrowded as the little gathering sat around the desk, waiting for Mrs. Langfeld to begin.

"Before I start," she said, "I want to make it clear that, at the moment, all this is *strictly* confidential and should not be passed on to anyone. Probably most of this information will be disclosed at the trial, but until then, discretion is of the utmost importance." She glanced down at the papers in her hand and, half reading from them, began to furnish her audience with the facts.

"Gerald Campbell—otherwise known as Gerhardt Wollter—was indeed, as he claims, born in Scotland, in the year 1897. His father, who was a German named Konrad Wollter, met Gerald's mother, Winifred Campbell, while on holiday in Scotland and married her in 1895, deciding to settle down in the pleasant Highland surroundings. To please Winifred's family, who were not too fond of foreigners, he adopted his wife's surname and when their son was born they registered him as Gerald Campbell. At school, young Gerald's academic achievements were nothing spectacular and his headmaster, now elderly and retired, remembers him as a boy who was often bullied and occasionally flew into violent rages. As he grew older, he in turn, would bully the younger boys. When Gerald was sixteen, his father decided he had had enough of Scotland and returned to Germany with his wife and son, reverting to the name Wollter and registering Gerald as Gerhardt. The boy continued his schooling there but, although he picked up German quickly, he failed to qualify for University and went through a series of unsatisfying jobs. In 1920 he joined the German army, where he seemed to thrive.

"In 1925 his father died, having been injured fighting in

the first World War, and his mother decided to return to Britain. Gerald did not go with her, preferring to stay in Germany. When Winifred died, four years later, he did go to Scotland to attend the funeral and then went to Somerset to spend the rest of his leave with an old classmate. There he met and married Emily Foster, taking her back to Germany with him.

"When Hitler, *yimach shemo*, rose to power, Gerald was one of his staunch supporters. It is unclear what his actual activities were during the war...the investigators are still trying to ascertain the information, but I think it is pretty certain what they were!" There were nods of agreement and murmurs from the gathering in the office. "It seems," Mrs. Langfeld continued, "that, as soon as the Allies marched in and liberated the concentration camps, the Campbells or, shall I say, the Wollters made a quick getaway. Where they went is unknown. It is surmised they spent over a year lying low somewhere in South America. There are records of them returning to England in November 1946, using their British names and passports."

"Where did they live before they moved here?" Mrs. Gold asked, when Mrs. Langfeld paused for breath.

"Apparently, they traveled around a bit," the headmistress went on, placing the file on her desk, "mostly in the big cities. But they realized it was a bit dangerous, as many Jews or other refugees were settling in the main towns and so they decided they would be safer in some little village in the countryside.

"They bought the house next door because it was cheap, not bothered that it was next to a school. They were quite shocked when they visited me and discovered it was a *Jewish* school! Mr. Campbell was determined to get us out of the way. Pretending to be friendly, he tried to find out what he could about us and then made every effort to have the school closed. He even used the discovery of the bomb as a means to discredit us. Once he overheard our German conversation, Miss Zemmel, and found out that I'd handled the bomb, he sought to convince the authorities that I was too irresponsible to run a school."

"How dare he!" Etty interrupted, causing a ripple of laughter.

Mrs. Langfeld smiled and carried on. "Then, when that didn't work, he changed his tactics altogether. His aim was to hound us out, hence the anti-Semitic slogans."

"*Ach* so!" Miss Zemmel commented, comprehending.

"He pursued his campaign with various tricks, trying to goad three girls into eating *treifa* cake…complaining about the noise…anything to make me feel I must move the school away, lock stock and barrel."

"Well, I'm glad you stood your ground and didn't give in to it!" Etty piped up. "It would have been awful to move away from here!"

Fortunately, no one noticed the secretive glance that passed between Mrs. Langfeld and Mrs. Gold—or their faint smiles of amusement.

"Well, that's it then," Mrs. Langfeld said and gathered up the papers neatly, clipping them together and placing them in a drawer, which she locked firmly. She stood up. "I think I'll take a day off tomorrow and go down to London to visit your mother, Nechy. I'd like to give her the gist of this report."

"Oh!" A worried frown crossed the girl's face. "Should I come with you?"

"No, I don't think so. You've only just come back, so it's not necessary."

After the showdown at Mr. Campbell's cottage, Mrs. Langfeld had suggested Nechy accompany her mother back to London and stay with her for a few days.

"She's a lot better now," Nechy had reported when she returned. "She still seems a bit shaken and her nights are quite disturbed, but she keeps saying she has to pick herself up and carry on with her life. In fact, she's sort of...more positive, somehow, than she was."

Yet, now, knowing what Mrs. Langfeld was going to talk to her mother about, Nechy could not help feeling concerned.

"Do you think she'll be able to take it?" she asked.

"Don't worry," the headmistress reassured her. "I'll tread carefully. If I see it upsets her, I'll stop. But it's only fair to tell her the full story, tat is if she does want to know it. In any case, she knows the more horrible parts—she witnessed all of it, after all."

"Y...yes," Nechy said, slowly, agreeing after a moment's consideration. "And she'll be pleased to see you. I know there's something she wants to discuss with you."

A
STRONGER BOND

"OH, HERE YOU ARE, SHULAMIS. MRS. LANGFELD wants to see you in her office." Yocheved poked her head round the door of Form Daled classroom, where Shulamis was sorting out her books, deciding which ones to take with her for the summer.

An anxious look crossed Shulamis's face. "What does she want me for?" she asked nervously.

"I wouldn't know," Yocheved replied. "But don't look so worried. She wasn't wearing her stern expression so I don't think you're in trouble."

Shulamis closed her desk immediately and made her way to the headmistress's office, feeling extremely apprehensive. What could Mrs. Langfeld want to speak to her about? She didn't think it had anything to do with her school work, as her exam results had been quite satisfactory. Perhaps it was something to do with the fact that she was going to spend the summer with Nechy and Mrs. Horowitz.

Her heart sank as a thought suddenly occurred to her.

She knew what it was! Mrs. Langfeld was going to suggest she go somewhere else, letting Nechy be alone with her mother for a bit. And she would be quite right, too! Why hadn't she thought of it herself, instead of experiencing the embarrassment of having someone point it out to her?

She knocked timidly on the office door and, in reply to Mrs. Langfeld's "come in," entered diffidently.

"Ah, Shulamis!" the headmistress's tone was warm and welcoming. "Come in. There is something I would like to talk to you about."

Relaxing a little, though still puzzled, Shulamis sat down on the chair Mrs. Langfeld indicated and waited for her to begin.

"You're going to the Horowitz's house for the summer, aren't you?" Mrs. Langfeld said at last.

There it was. She had been right after all!

"Yes, I was," she said hurriedly, attempting to save face by getting her say in quickly, "but Yitty Lieber invited me and I think I should go to her so that Nechy can have some time alone with her mother."

"No, Shulamis, I don't think you're right. Both Mrs. Horowitz and Nechy are looking forward to having you there. I've just been to see Mrs. Horowitz and she told me so. In fact, that is what I want to talk to you about." She paused and scrutinized Shulamis thoughtfully. Wondering what was coming, the girl looked up expectantly and felt apprehensive to hear what Mrs. Langfeld would say.

But, instead of explaining herself, the headmistress continued with a question.

"Shulamis, could you look upon Mrs. Horowitz as your mother?" she asked.

"W-what do you mean?" Shulamis stammered, perplexed. "Why do you ask me that?"

"I'll explain in a minute. Just answer my question, if you can. Your reply is quite important."

Shulamis considered the matter earnestly for a moment. "I don't know," she said presently. "I don't really know what one feels toward a mother. I don't remember my mother at all."

"I see." The unexpected response took Mrs. Langfeld by surprise, but, seeing the bewildered look on the girl's face, she hastened to enlighten her.

"When I spoke to Mrs. Horowitz last week she told me that she would like very much to adopt you, if you would agree to it. How do you feel about the idea?"

Shulamis could only stare at her, dumbfounded. Adopted? To have a home to go to? She had stopped dreaming about that a long time ago. Without thinking, she asked, "But what about Nechy? Who says she would want to share her mother with me?"

"Nechy knows about it and she's absolutely thrilled with the idea. There has always been a strong bond between the two of you, hasn't there? And now, since all that has happened, it has become stronger than ever. Am I right?"

Shulamis nodded silently. She was dazed. Her emotions were in a swirl. A home! A place to call her own! No longer would she have to be shuffled from place to place for holidays! No longer would she wonder who would be nice enough to invite her for the summer.

"Well," Mrs. Langfeld went on, "now you can become real sisters! And you will have someone who you could come to love as a mother at last!"

Shulamis, still speechless, found her mind wandering back to her conversation with Mrs. Horowitz on the day she had moved. Snatches of it came back to her. "I wish you really were sisters...Nechy needs a sister...to replace the one she had..." And then, she had given her that strange look. Was that when the idea had come to her? Shulamis suddenly felt engulfed in a feeling of warmth. Of course it would be completely wonderful to have a mother and a sister...and a home. But wouldn't she always feel like an intruder? She was in a quandary, not sure what to say, and her face eloquently expressed her dilemma.

"You don't have to give your answer yet," Mrs. Langfeld assured her gently, watching Shulamis in her emotional turmoil. "See how you feel when you have spent some time together with them. But don't take too long deciding, because the legal proceedings can take a long time."

Legal proceedings! It all seemed so official and binding. Was it what she really wanted? To acquire a new family? It had its attractions...if only she could be sure she was really wanted!

Holiday time, at last! Migdal Binoh closed its doors for the next five weeks, amid shouts of goodbye—some tearful and some happy and excited—as girls scrambled onto the hired buses carrying them off in different directions. Nechy and Shulamis sat together, closer than ever, hugging their unspoken secret to themselves. Nechy had only broached the subject once, after Mrs. Langfeld had spoken to Shulamis, but, understanding that she must give her friend time to make up her mind, had kept quiet after that.

However, it was enough to convince Shulamis that there would be absolutely no resentment on Nechy's part if she accepted. On the contrary—Nechy welcomed the idea. She not only needed support in taking care of her mother, but she felt so close to Shulamis. It seemed only right that after all the years they had spent as orphans together, that they now both have a home together.

All the same, Shulamis could not quite rid herself of the feeling that she might be intruding. Every summer she had gone somewhere else—always feeling like a burden; here she was actually *wanted*, yet it remained so hard for her to believe.

She was still of two minds as the Liebers' car dropped them outside the house in which Mrs. Horowitz's flat was situated. What if I still can't make up my mind by the time the holidays are over? she worried. Nevertheless, as Nechy and Shulamis hurried up the stairs, dragging their bulging suitcases, Shulamis had a strange feeling that she was coming home!

Mrs. Horowitz flung the door open wide, a welcoming smile on her face, her blue-green eyes sparkling with happiness. She drew them inside, hugging and kissing them both warmly.

The flat looked pleasant and homey and the girls looked round it appreciatively, happy to be home at last. Then they noticed something that warmed their hearts even more. The dining room door was ajar and to their surprise, there, on the table, was the beautifully embroidered cream-linen tablecloth, its red poppies and yellow sunflowers brightly lit by the late afternoon sunlight streaming in from the window.

GLOSSARY

Please note: All the words in this glossary
are Hebrew, unless otherwise noted.

Agudah—lit., congregation; worldwide organization
Aleichem Shalom—lit., unto you, peace; hello; response to
Shalom Aleichem
Bashert (Yiddish)—predestined
Bentched (Yiddish)—recited Grace after Meals, the prayer
said after eating bread
Bentchers (Yiddish)—booklet containing the bentching, or
Grace after Meals prayer
Beruchim habaim—welcome
Bitochon—trust; refers to trust in G-d
Boruch Hashem—thank G-d
Bris—circumcision
Chamisho Oser B'Shvat—the fifteenth day of the month
of Shvat (the eleventh month in the Jewish calendar year)

commonly known as Tu B'Shvat

Chanukah—a Jewish holiday celebrating the Maccabees' victory over the Greeks

Chas veshalom—G-d forbid

Chasunah—wedding

Cheder—religious elementary school

Chillul Hashem—desecration of G-d's name

Chizuk—strength; usually referring to emotional strength

Chumash—Bible

Daled—the fourth letter of the Hebrew alphabet, with a numerical value of four

Daven—pray

Der Leiber G-tt (Yiddish or German)—the beloved G-d

Dovid Hamelech—King David

Du bisst ehr (German)—you are the person!

Du lügst (German)—you are lying

Fleishig (Yiddish or German)—food containing meat

Gam zu letovah—this is also good

Gemillas Chesed—acts of kindness

Hatzlachah—success

Im yirtzeh Hashem—lit., if G-d wants

Kever Rochel—the grave of the matriarch Rachel

Koach—strength

Lag B'omer—lit., thirty-third day of the Omer; Jewish holiday

Lager (Yiddish or German)—term used to refer to a concentration camp

Mazel Tov—congratulations

Mensch—lit., man; upstanding individual

Minchah—afternoon prayer

Mizrach—east

Mohel—a person who performs circumcisions

Motzoei Shabbos—Saturday night, after Sabbath has

ended

Negel vasser (Yiddish)—lit., water for the nails; the ritual washing of the hands first thing in the morning

Nein (Yiddish or German)—no

Oy, Mamme! Mamme—oh, Mommy! Mommy!

Pesach—Passover

Purim—Jewish holiday that comes one month before Passover

Rav—esteemed Rabbi

Ribono Shel Olam—Master of the world

Roshah—wicked person

Schlepp—drag

Schrecklich (German)—terrible

Seudoh—festive meal

Shabbos—Sabbath

Shalom Aleichem—lit., peace be unto you; hello

Sheitel (Yiddish)—wig

Shevuos—Jewish holiday

Shalom Zachor—party on the Sabbath following the birth of a baby boy

Sifrei Tehillim—books of Psalms

Simchah—celebration

Siyata dishmaya—heavenly assistance

Tehillim—Psalms

Treifa—lit., torn; not kosher

Tzitzis—four cornered fringed garment worn by Jewish males

Vov—the sixth letter of the Hebrew alphabet, with a numerical value of six

Wuss tit ehr du? (Yiddish)—what is he doing here?

Yarmulka—skull cap worn by Jewish males

Yeshiva bochur—Jewish boy attending religious high school and post high school

Yiddish—Jewish; common language used by many Jews
Yiden (Yiddish)—Jews
Yimach shemo—may his name be erased
Yom Kippur—Day of Atonement
Yom Tov—Jewish holiday
Zeichnet sehr gut (German)—draws very well